The

Fisherman's

Bride

The Untold Story of the Wife of Simon Peter

A Novel by

Catherine Magia

ISBN-13: 978-1540310446

ISBN-10: 1540310442

Cover photo by Paul Nguyen
Headshot by Jack Turkel

FOR MY MOTHER,
WHOSE LOVE OF STORYTELLING INSPIRED THIS
TALE

PROLOGUE

You only know of me through the healing of my mother, a shadow of a woman blessed by a miracle in the Gospels of Luke, Mark, and Matthew. I did not merit a footnote; indeed, I did not even have a name in these accounts. I reside in the silence, the space between the stories, a whispering in the wind. My name has become dust. It has scattered so far from the golden ledges of Mount Tabor, drifted so far from the writhing branches of Gethsemane, buried so deep under the scintillating tides of Galilee, that I no longer remember it. My name does not matter. I was a woman in love with a man named Simon. I was married to the martyr, the proverbial rock, the first pope, when he was only a man. A part of Simon Peter belonged to me.

There was also another: Jesus. When he called to me, he awakened something beyond the binds of mortality, beyond flesh and skin. It was the memory of light, an exquisite and perfect love embedded within the soul. He taught me to discover the raw material of divinity within the self. He taught that sin splinters the soul, and that we are broken, shards of our own darkness weighing us down.

To soar, we must forsake the self and allow it to die, as he died. I did not come without a struggle. Indeed, few of us do.

Come, I invite you to walk with me.

CHAPTER I

I did not know who was coming. My mother had excused me from my daily weaving duties and asked me to oversee Leta, our slave, in the kitchen. We prepared barley beer. We placed fresh bougainvillea and bellflowers in water bowls, their scents intoxicating. My father was expecting an important guest, and it felt odd to have him home. He was usually absent during the day, contracting with merchants and negotiating orders until the markets closed. He rarely dined until long after the sun had set. Only when the sky had faded into darkness did I know my father would be home.

Everything had been made ready, and while still in the kitchen, I heard a man's voice, thick with a foreign accent. As he enunciated his words, I also noted a roughness to his tone. Then my father's baritone rang out in welcome, smooth and polished as onyx. The men exchanged pleasantries, and their conversation then went right to business: to numbers, labor, and profit. Soon enough, my father's throaty laughter rumbled, followed by an invitation for the guest to join him for barley beer.

My mother had already prepared a tray with beer jugs and handed it to me.

"Serve them with care," she said, but her expression contained warning enough for me.

I nodded, pleased to be entrusted with the task. In prior years whenever my father entertained, my mother typically sent me away or confined me to my chamber. I'd always only heard stories of banquets and fascinating guests secondhand from Leta. Even though she was a slave, Leta and I shared confidences like sisters. I'd always envied her observances of my father's table, when I myself had been prohibited from attending. Now, with the beer tray in hand, I smiled to myself and left the kitchen.

"Ah...here she is," Father remarked.

I kept my head tilted down, my eyes fixed on the pitcher as I poured the barley beer into two jugs. Without meaning to do so, I filled one jug higher than the other. The guest took the jug overflowing with beer and jerked it toward his mouth. A small splash dribbled all the way down onto his neck.

"This is Hasar," my father said, "the most prosperous fish merchant in Capernaum—and my partner."

I bowed, keeping my gaze low.

When I glimpsed a flamboyant mantle set with jeweled hues, my father added, "He is Egyptian."

Hasar's nose was bulbous, and he had a plebeian face, with a high forehead due to a receding hairline. His black eyebrows were slanted like a hawk's wing, giving him a startled expression.

As he sloshed down more beer, I looked down again

before he could catch me studying him.

In turn, though, Hasar perused me as he might a scroll—memorizing my color, my shape, my size, it seemed. My hands suddenly grew clammy. I wiped my palms at the sides of my apron, and I felt a blush creeping onto my cheeks.

"Look at me, my dear," Hasar said to me.

I stared at the ground, the floor that my father had hoped to someday cover with marble. My heart trembled, a faint fluttering of doom, and I had no desire to scrutinize Hasar's face. I wished I could disappear.

"Daughter, you must not have heard. Our guest commands you to lift your head."

There was warning in my father's voice.

When I complied, I saw a swarthy man whose impatient eyes surveyed me as he would a cow or an expensive carpet. He assessed my height and diminutive stature, wisps of dark hair that managed to escape from my head scarf, and my deep-set eyes, said to resemble lapis lazuli. Then his eyes glossed over me and surveyed everything else in the room. I tried to imagine a spark of emotion in those eyes. I found that I could not.

"Daughter, we are hungry. Fetch us our meal."

"Yes, Father."

In the kitchen, my mother and Leta had prepared an abundance of olives, figs, and pomegranates on the prized pewter dishes that we rarely used. As I passed back and forth from the kitchen, I heard my father enumerating my

9

attributes. I knew what that meant and felt my heart begin to pound, but I tried not to think about it and forced myself to focus on my work.

"She seems willful." Hasar sounded annoyed.

My father gave a nervous laugh. "She is young."

"She is very skillful with her loom. Her mother comes from a long tradition of weavers, and she has passed those secrets down to our daughter."

Hasar grunted in reply.

Then I brought out the steaming fried carp, lightly spiced with lemon juice and coriander. Hasar smiled after he caught a whiff of the seductive aroma wafting from my mother's most coveted dish. My father watched him all the while, I noticed.

"Her talents in the kitchen are unparalleled," Father said. "She has learned well from her mother."

I raised my eyebrows slightly, but my father looked away. He did not often lie.

I gathered up the empty plates and refilled their jugs until they were brimming with barley beer. Then I realized that my father and Hasar had stopped talking and now looked up. I felt my jaw tighten. Both stared at me with amused expressions, as if sharing a delicious joke.

Later, when I had just departed from the room, I heard Hasar chuckle.

"Yes, my friend," Father said, "she will give you many sons. Like my own wife."

I felt my heart thudding all the way into my throat.

After Hasar had left, my father called me. I waited for some time before I answered. He remained seated, drinking barley beer despite the departure of his guest. My father seemed exuberant, his face pink and flickering with pride.

"Hasar has agreed. You two will be married by the new moon." He clapped his hands.

I pressed my lips together.

"Do not look at me like that, daughter." My father frowned. "I am providing well for you. Hasar is one of the wealthiest men in these parts. After the marriage, we will form an alliance with my fishing and his processing industries. I will have a monopoly on supplying fish to his retinue and my revenues will essentially double."

I ignored his talk and asked, "Is he a good man, Abba?"

He paused, then said, "He is a successful man. He rose from nothing, the son of foreign slaves."

"He seems … brusque." I tried to keep the reproach out of my voice.

"It is an advantageous match." My father nodded, tapping the table with his knuckles. "Best offer of marriage you'll ever get. Besides, marriage is not just about you. It is the union of two families, of businesses."

He stood up deliberately and his height felt intimidating. I knew the conversation had ended. My father was Ephraim, proprietor of a large fishing business, and he was not accustomed to his orders being questioned.

"All that needs to be discussed now is the bride-price."

His words washed over me like cold water. My chest tightened even as my heart raced. I could not think of anything to say. I could only run.

———

I ran to the sea. The sea was my salvation. The Sea of Galilee mirrored the early-evening sun, a blue iridescence that blinded the eye. Across the horizon, seagulls filled the air with predatory calls. Fishing nets lay drying on the shore. In a wicker basket, frenzied fish leapt back and forth, blinking like a hundred silver coins. A tall, lanky shadow caught the corner of my eye, and I drew in a deep breath.

"Is it not a bit early for you to be here?"

Simon stood before me, smiling his crooked smile. His eyes were a slate gray, the color of the sea during a storm. He had paused while pulling nets from the boat onto the shore, one foot wading in the water and the other foot on sand. The boat had not been anchored, causing him to continually skirt backward and making him look rather ridiculous.

I laughed.

Simon was the oldest of my father's four apprentices.

He was not as fine featured as John, or as rugged and robust as James. Neither was he as meticulous and exacting in details as his brother, Andrew. Simon had a buoyant spirit, a strong sense of camaraderie, and a penchant for exploration. It was Simon who suggested using hooks to fish in addition to nets, supplementing the catch with a surplus. It was also Simon who forgot to clean the hooks properly, causing the rust to distort the metal curvatures.

Simon had been working for my father the longest, and my father trusted his ability to navigate the sea and scour for the largest fish. From the day he arrived, Simon never spoke to me as if I were a child. Despite being eight years my senior, he praised my natural curiosity and answered my questions with patience. We explored the whole of Capernaum together, watching the caravans come and go towards Jerusalem. Simon and I, we were co-conspirators in the quest for adventure. I would return home, hollyhock in my hair, grass stains on my tunic, and scratches on my knees. My mother would reprimand me and I would barely hear her, enraptured in my own dreams.

Simon also liked to tell me where I came from. He told me stories of Jacob and his laborious servitude for seven years to win the lovely Rachel … the Egyptian prince Moses … and the divinely empowered David, who defeated the giant Goliath. He did not shy away from stories with violence, nor from stories of crimes and retribution of human passion. He revered the imminent struggle of our people, and our ability to overcome. So I believed in the ancient tales. I learned that blood was sometimes the price for peace and that love did not always end happily.

After I finished my weaving or spinning for the day, I would often run out to see Simon. We always met at the same place, where the water gathered in an opalescent pool along a narrow ridge of sand. I was usually elated to watch Simon lowering the sails and anchoring the boat as dusk settled. I rarely came early. So he knew by my face that something was amiss now.

"What is wrong?" he asked, taking my hands in his.

I shook my head and stared at the sea, sighing.

"Sighs are as bad as tears." Simon said as he studied me.

"You are not supposed to be back at the shore yet," I said.

He shrugged. "My net broke. I decided I would haul the fish baskets to the marketplace while back at shore. I am pleased, or else I would not meet you here. What is troubling you?" He eyed me.

I took a deep breath. "I am to be married."

Simon grinned. The fact seemed to amuse him—not the response I had hoped for.

"Well, how old are you?" he asked.

"Fifteen."

"Mm, then I would say it is time."

All my frustration, anger, and fears culminated in that moment. A rush of hot tears sprang to my eyes, feelings I did not know I had, and I yanked my hands from Simon's and swung blindly at him. I did not mean to slap him, but I saw the red mark on his cheek and stopped.

"I am sorry."

Simon caught my hands in his again.

I refused to look at him.

"Has your father chosen your husband?"

I nodded, my eyes still downcast.

"It is Hasar the fish merchant."

Simon did not respond, and I peeked upward at him. He seemed to be deliberating. At length, he stroked my fingers and spoke quietly. "Do you think you will be happy?"

"He … he seems a cruel man."

Simon gave a slow nod. "He is. I have seen Hasar with his slaves and his laborers. He has little compassion and even less patience for those under his supervision … and, I would imagine, in his household."

We sat down together in silence, my head immediately resting upon his shoulder. Gradually, the western sky pulsed with light and our silhouettes appeared on the ground before us, linked through the arms. Then our shadows dissolved into the darkness as the sun faded beneath the earth. I clasped Simon tighter, to ensure he was still there amidst the bustle of other fishermen working along the shore in the soft glimmer of lantern light.

"How…" Simon whispered, and then cleared his throat. "How would your father respond if another suitor vied for your hand?"

"Well…" I considered the possibility. "He would have to choose, I suppose. But how would that be different from now? He has already chosen."

"The difference is," Simon answered, his eye glinting in the lantern light, "you can have a voice in choosing the man you marry if there is another. That has been the tradition since Rebekah consented to become the wife of Isaac."

And he kissed me.

Simon never told me that he loved me, but I never doubted that he did. I knew by the tenderness of his lips and the way he touched my neck, brushing strands of hair that fell onto my skin. I knew by the way he cupped my chin and how his fingers sought to memorize the fullness of my cheek. I saw myself in his inquisitive eyes—and I was beautiful.

―――――

I must have been glowing as I rushed home, and I felt sure no one noticed. Mother waited for me at the door, her eyes wide and anxious. I prayed my father was not waiting.

"Where have you been?" she demanded.

"At the fishing dock."

"What were you doing? It is after dark. We almost

sent a search party after you." Her reproach sounded fraught with worry. I had never been gone this long without a shomrim.

"Thinking."

My mother was not fooled. She saw my uplifted face, and she immediately looked suspicious. Her left eye twitched slightly and she curled her lip in thought. My mother was a quiet woman and she expressed everything through small gestures.

"Whom were you with?"

"Simon." I could not suppress a smile.

My mother stifled a gasp, and she dragged me back to my bedchamber, bolting the door. I did not think she could move so quickly. She sat down across from me on the woolen mattress, clutching my hands in a severe grip. My wrists throbbed and I thought of Simon's soft touch, his fleshy palms.

"Did you lie with him?" she asked.

I jerked back, and I felt my eyes grow wide. "What? No."

"Truly?"

"No!" I pulled away. "Simon is an honorable man."

She let out a held breath. Her face softened like the melting of butter, and her clear eyes looked sad. When she spoke again, her tone seemed sympathetic.

"Daughter, I know that Simon is your dearest friend. However, now that you are promised to Hasar, you must conduct yourself with the proper etiquette." She lowered her voice and said, "Women have been stoned for indecent behavior. You must be cautious."

I squared my shoulders. "I am not going to marry Hasar. I will marry Simon."

My mother just gazed at me. It was the first time I had disobeyed her.

"Your father… He has already given his promise. Hasar is making preparations for the bride-price and the wedding. Your father is planning a celebration banquet."

I shook my head. Tears brimmed in the corners of my eyes. "I love Simon," I said simply.

I waited for her to resist. I waited for her brow to crease in disappointment. I waited for the scolding, the torrent of coldness to resonate in her manner toward me until I had surrendered. I imagined my father's volatile temper, harsh words, and chains locking my chamber door until I came to my senses. I waited for a storm that never came.

Instead, my mother put her delicate fingers on my forehead. Slowly, she tousled my hair until it came loose from my head scarf—dark locks tumbled onto my shoulders, resembling her own tresses.

"A woman's greatest gamble is her choice of a husband," she said. "Ours is not an easy life, surviving against weather and the constant harassment of tax collectors. Your father and I have spent many years building a sustainable life. We struggled at first." Mother paused here, then went on. "Your brothers will inherit the

18

fishing enterprise after your father's death. Women must be practical. Hasar is well established and his fish-processing business is steadily growing. He is also friendly with the Romans. Being a merchant, he could offer you comfort, luxurious foods, and travel to distant lands. You will be well cared for, which is my dearest wish for you, my little one."

I nodded and looked down. I thought of Reuben, tall and lanky, preoccupied with matters of consequence as befit the eldest son of the family. Levi was younger by two years, yet he was in fierce competition with Reuben over my father's affection. Levi was industrious in his studies, and even more determined to learn my father's business. I rarely saw either of my brothers, as they were perpetual shadows of Ephraim himself, and it was common knowledge that both sons would linger on either side of the master fisherman wherever he was present. I doubted if either would consider my welfare.

"Simon…" she said. "He is one of your father's apprentices and he is virtually penniless. He is an orphan. He has no family pedigree, no property. What could he offer you?" I heard a note of pleading in her voice.

I did not know how to answer. I sat before my mother as if on trial, and the sentence would be my future. I only knew that I belonged to Simon and he belonged to me. Our souls were intertwined from the first mountain he helped me climb, the first time my hand brushed against his. For an instant, I imagined waking in the same bed as

Hasar, his dark impatient eyes darker than the night. I cringed.

"Himself, Amah. Simon could offer me himself."

"You have not made a wise choice."

She shook her head and murmured, more to herself than to me. Then she did a surprising thing. Perhaps it was the insistence in my voice, or the tears streaming down my cheeks. Or, perhaps, she had made such a choice in her past and it left her marriage lacking. I never knew why my parents spoke so little to each other. She held me in her bosom, rocking back and forth. It harkened back to the days when I sought her breast whenever I fell or skinned my knees.

———

The night of the betrothal banquet arrived. I wondered why my mother had not yet told my father about Simon — I knew she had asked to see Simon in private, but Simon had not divulged anything to me. He had been busy after long days of fishing, negotiating new anchors with stonemasons, and mending the broken nets. He was also bargaining with linen merchants for new sails. Even when I saw him at the dock, he seemed too exhausted to talk.

Mother taught me to wait until time ripened like a sweet fruit. She had asked me to play the part of the subservient daughter. But I could not wait any longer. Tonight, Father and Hasar would negotiate the marriage covenant and agree upon the bride-price. Unlike Jewish youths who needed a deputy or father to speak upon their behalf, Hasar had dismissed the need for a friend of the bridegroom and elected to speak for himself. Father had agreed to this breach of custom, considering Hasar's maturity and his success. Tonight's festivities would be my undoing. Once consent and agreement upon the bride-price were publicly obtained, the contract would be sealed with a toast by a drink made of roasted grain. This night would bind me to Hasar. After the ceremony, I would legally become his betrothed. There would be no escape.

I wondered when Simon would come for me. The guests began filtering into my father's house, and I could see them by peeking behind the door. My heart fluttered every time the door opened. Every shuffling footstep sent blood to my cheeks.

Hasar had come early, now conversing with my father. He was bedecked in Egyptian finery of azure and gold; a stunning headdress wrapped around his brow like a turban. My father, though more modestly dressed, looked distinguished in a tunic of pale linen. My brothers, Levi and Reuben, stood beside him, awkward in formal tunics instead of their usual fishing vestments.

My mother came to help me dress, bringing the wedding garments she had worn a generation ago. They were the most splendid I had ever seen. The outer garment was a deep wine red. The tunic was a white so fine it appeared transparent, edged with silver beading. The veil looked particularly beautiful, embroidered with many colors and lined with gold thread. I would wear it before the night concluded. Customarily, the bride's attire at the betrothal feast paled in comparison to the wedding feast, but my mother took painstaking care in preparing the grandest for me. I was unlikely to have a wedding feast if I married Simon. I looked at my mother, imploring news of Simon. I mouthed inaudible words, fearful of servants lingering at the doorways with watchful eyes.

She shook her head.

"My darling," she whispered, "do not speak. Drink from your chosen cup."

I nodded while she arranged the headdress, which was shaped like a triangle. She drew lines of kohl around my eyes, shaded them with terra-cotta, and then smiled into the mirror. My mother kissed my forehead, her tears wetting the plain beneath my eye. She then covered me in sparkling baubles and threaded daisies in my hair, gently pushing me out.

Many guests had gathered in my father's house, a jubilant crowd in their fine clothes. A hush fell over them as my mother guided me to my father, who stood by a small table, looking very pleased. The marriage contract lay on the table, signed with Hasar's steady hand. The fish merchant smiled as I approached, and I noticed that his teeth were sharp and angular.

"Honored guests," my father began, "we are gathered here today to witness the betrothal of my daughter to Hasar the fish merchant. I have reviewed the marriage contract, and I find it satisfactory. The bride-price is also exceedingly generous. We will be proud to call this prosperous man our son."

Hasar nodded, as if on cue. I suddenly remembered his opaque past, his flair for theatrics and the rumors of his travels with magicians and pagans. His words were honeyed and he spoke deliberately: "To the bride's family, I present five camels, in the tradition of Isaac and Rebekah. Each camel is laden with a different gift: salt, spices, silk, exotic fruits, and a casket of gold jewelry."

Five servants of Hasar stepped forward in turn, each carrying a silken pillow, upon which a symbolic fraction of the treasures rested. The crowd gasped at his ostentatious show of wealth. Even Reuben and Levi seemed impressed. According to tradition, the number of camels denoted the worth of the bride. One camel was considered a trifling, while five camels were the epitome of honor, the highest a maiden could hope to command. I wondered what my father had promised Hasar to procure such generous terms. My mother raised her eyebrows at me. I understood her meaning: I still had time to choose this life.

A proud girl unveiled the twinkling gold rings, their glitter and her greed reflected in her dark eyes. Pomegranates lay in the arms of the second servant girl, round fruit matching her rounded arms, and Hasar reached over to grab the fruit, breaking the skin and spilling blood-like seeds over the cushion. The third servant girl was masked, the lower half of her face covered by a swath of fabric so airy and luxurious it could only be the finest of silk. She carried many folds of the same dazzling cloth, spilling around her elbows like a waterfall. I could smell the fourth servant before she stepped forward, the frankincense and myrrh emanating from her hair as much as from the twin bowls in her grasp. The final servant girl was only a child, her fingers trembling as crystals of salt tumbled from her jar onto the ground.

Hasar flinched. His cape swept toward the spilled salt, and in an instant, the salt jar had been overturned on the hearth. His eyes narrowed at his servants and he moved toward the little girl, his cape expanding to hide her, like a hawk unfurling its wings and revealing its talons. The child quickly ducked under his cape and hurried toward the elder servants, but I saw a slight red mark upon her cheek, the impact of a hand upon her soft face, and reddened with pomegranate juice—a slap of shame. Hasar's eyes now appeared satisfied as she quickly crept away.

Father, meanwhile, seemed impatient. "Pour the wine," he ordered.

I could not lift my eyes from Hasar's fingers, stained from the pomegranate juice. Then a servant placed a chalice before me, its contents blood-red, the red blinding. I stared into the wine and imagined myself drowning.

Then I saw him—Simon, crossing the threshold of the doorway. He had donned a red tunic of fine material and it ended at his knee, unlike the long tunics worn by all the other men. He had shaved, and his hair, usually wild as brambles in the thickets, had been tamed by a comb. He carried a rolled parchment and a pouch of camel skin.

A delicious warmth spread over me, and I knew who would be my husband.

"Wait!" Simon said.

Father turned. "Simon, my loyal apprentice," he said. "You are most welcome to attend the banquet. However, I trust you will not disturb the proceedings of my daughter's betrothal."

Simon bowed, his expression resolute when he looked at my father. "Master, I have not come to attend the ceremony. I have come to present your daughter with an offer of marriage."

I saw Father offer a wide, but forced, smile. "We are honored by your intentions, but my daughter will marry Hasar." Despite his jovial expression, my father's eyes seemed devoid of emotion. He looked Simon up and down, noting the shorter length of his tunic, a subtle reminder of his station.

I took a step forward. "I have not consented yet, Abba."

Now Father peered at me. "After you drink from this chalice, you will become Hasar's wife. Drink, my daughter."

My father held the cup toward me. I made no move to accept it.

I took a breath. "I beg you to consider Simon's offer,"

I said, faster than I had meant to.

Father, though, appeared immovable; the smile remained on his lips. Only the way he clenched the chalice betrayed his anger toward me.

"You are my daughter, and you will obey me in this." His voice held a clear warning.

"Husband," my mother said gently. "Our daughter is fifteen now."

"Indeed," said the wizened rabbi Jesophat, "a girl is free to determine for herself after twelve and a half years. According to the Talmud, a woman can be acquired only with her consent and not without it. Rebekah, you recall, was asked if she wanted to follow Isaac."

My father's face turned ashen. He knew he had been cornered. His guests and neighbors would judge him if he tried to coerce me to his will now. His expression like iron, he placed the chalice back onto the table with a contemplative expression.

"Our daughter has been honored by more than one suitor," my mother continued in soft, persuasive tones. "It cannot hurt to review another marriage contract."

His pursed lips and clenched jaw told me of his reluctance, but he finally unrolled and glanced through the parchment brought by Simon. Folding his arms, Father glared at Simon, with thinly veiled contempt.

The apprentice faced his master squarely.

"What do you propose for a bride-price?" Father asked.

Simon gave a slight bow of his head. "Master, I learned my trade from you and will always be indebted to you. However, I have begun my own fishing business. From this day forth, I will no longer be your apprentice, but I will surrender half my profits to you until I leave the sea."

My father laughed. "Compared to Hasar's proposal, you offer trifles. What use will that be to me?"

"Very little, at first," Simon said. "However, as my business grows, so will your revenues. I was your apprentice; you must have faith in what you taught me."

I saw my father stiffen at Simon's confident tone.

"What gifts did you bring my daughter?" Father asked.

I smiled at Simon shyly. He caught my eye and then looked at my mother. She gave a small nod.

"I am not a wealthy man. I have only the amulet my mother left me when she died."

Simon held out a chain. On it, hanging by a fine thread, was a small rose carved in olive wood.

"I am Simon, son of Jonah. I have been an orphan for many years. This is the only link I have to my past. I offer it to your daughter, as I offer all of my humble self."

I trembled as Simon spoke these words; the sound of his assured voice echoed in my head. I longed to touch the rose—to place it upon my breast and to feel the smooth wood against my skin.

"Very well." My father waved his hand dismissively to

the guests. "Pour the wine."

A second chalice was filled with wine and then placed next to Simon's marriage covenant on the table. Despite my father's measured countenance, I saw his glowering eyes, which issued an unequivocal command. He turned his head slightly towards Hasar.

My father spoke in a strained voice. "Daughter, it is time to give your consent."

His lips were set in a grim line. He leaned forward and whispered so that only those standing close to him could hear: "Before you make your choice, daughter, be aware of this. If you drink from Simon's cup, you will no longer be welcome in this house. Your name will be stricken from our family's register."

My breath caught. "Abba…"

My eyes felt wild with confusion and fear as I looked at my mother. She flinched as if she had been struck by her husband's words.

Drawing in a sharp breath, I stared at the brimming cups, then up at my father standing next to Hasar, and Simon waiting patiently for me as he always did. Reuben and Levi looked at me with expectation, and I knew they would always follow my father's path. I hesitated as I reached out for Simon's cup, my hands trembling.

I swallowed the contents so hastily that I felt dizzy, heat rushing to my face, still swathed in the betrothal veil. The wine was warm in my throat, and my senses became sublimely heightened. I looked up at the wooden beams sustaining the ceiling with an odd sense of finality.

Simon came to my side. Slowly, he placed the amulet around my neck, his fingers fumbling. Then he spoke the words expected by tradition. "See by this token, you are set apart for me, according to the Law of Moses and of Israel."

He lifted the ethereal veil so all could see the face of his bride. Then he lowered it quickly, concealing the tears that I could no longer contain. The veil felt like a shroud.

My mother's eyes were melancholy as she stepped forward and embraced me, then gave me a celebratory kiss on both cheeks. Reuben and Levi shook their heads, mirror images of disappointment. The silence was overwhelming and shock pervaded the chamber like a heavy, oppressive breath. Steam from the prepared foods made it even more smothering. No one applauded. My father began to speak again, a great and thick rumbling that I could not decipher. Then someone in the crowd snickered, and the guests began murmuring and hissing. I knew the ceremony was finished.

I was now Simon's betrothed.

Hasar, meanwhile, glowered like an angry wolf, and I did not pity him. My father had turned away from me, and I could see only the pale mantle that matched his anger. So I was already forgotten. My name had become dust. No longer would I be remembered in family genealogies—an omission, a gap between the stories. I listened to the somber rhythm of my breathing, and yet to them, I was already dead.

CHAPTER II

And so I followed my husband. Although the Law prescribed a year for the groom to prepare a dwelling for his bride, I shared the same roof with Simon immediately. The sons of Jonah, Andrew and Simon lived together on the edge of Lake Gennesaret, where fisherman congregated at the highest point overlooking the water, over the sand dunes. He lived in a modest fishing hut with two rooms and a wooden ladder leading to the roof, which also served as the cooking quarters. Simon granted me the roof for my own chamber. It was an open space where light dripped like honey. I watched the constellations at night. The roof became my sanctuary.

Life with Simon, though, turned out to be more difficult than I had imagined.

My husband was poor. Here, the floor was dirt and the fireplace was a hollow in the dirt surrounded by stones. Simon and Andrew slept on mats woven from straw, reeds, and palm fronds, shrugging off the scratchiness as though it was a mere bug bite. I longed for the warmth of my goat-hair blankets, silken pillows, and smells of myrrh and frankincense from my father's vast house. The rooms here were profuse with the raw smell of fish, percolating from the brothers' tunics that I had not yet washed. They also had inadequate mosquito netting, and I was bloated with red obtrusions until I learned to douse myself in a foul-smelling ointment that kept the bloodthirsty gnats away. No doubt it would keep spouses away as well, and I spent hours washing myself to make myself desirable to my husband.

It was more than a month after the night of my betrothal and Simon still had not come to my bed. He had insisted on a celebration, however small, to legitimize our marriage even though it was already sealed by the rabbi Jesophat. My exile from the family of Ephraim the fisherman, proprietor of eight boats and twelve fishing stalls, rankled Simon like a wound that would not be mollified. The bride-price, which had not preserved my standing in the family, still had to be paid every year. He sought to vindicate himself and his wife, hoping our neighbors would be sympathetic to love. I reluctantly agreed.

———

I did not understand until I saw Leta. She was approaching the fishing village, carrying a large bundle and a knapsack. We embraced in a flood of tears, and I wiped her cheeks. My mother had sent her to live with me, along with a small sum of money for "provisions." I remonstrated her for following me into poverty, when she could enjoy the luxurious warmth of my father's fire. At the mention of

Abba, her eyes narrowed.

"Young mistress, your father let it be known far and wide that you are no longer his daughter. You have disobeyed and dishonored him. Your name is stricken from the family record, and the Master has dispatched a messenger to the Roman census headquarters declaring you dead. The bed you had once lain in has been burned, as have all your belongings. This is all I have salvaged."

The news was a blow to my heart, and my breath stopped. Leta handed me the satchel and the bundle. It all seemed so small, a life reduced to a knapsack and a bundle. I trembled as I thought of my grave, which would be without a family name, as I had no other name except that of my husband. Perhaps that, too, would be blotted out with time.

As I took the pack from her, she stepped backward and cringed.

I eyed her. "Let me see your hand."

Leta hesitated, then finally revealed her wrist. It was rife with bruises.

"I brought your spindle and your distaff—I know you must miss spinning." She nodded at the bundle in her left arm. "On the day they ransacked your chamber, I hid it from the others. Master discovered me."

Something inside me erupted: hot, volcanic anger. My father had never lashed a slave before. Sweet Leta, who bore the brunt of his rage with her skin and her loyalty. I unwrapped the pack, and twenty coins tumbled out into the sand. I picked up the money, then pressed it into her hands and held her close to my bosom.

"Leta, we cannot afford to feed you. Simon and I are struggling. We do not even have a floor of stone."

I felt ashamed to show her how we lived. Somehow, a wall had sprung between my old and new lives. I was no longer Ephraim's privileged daughter, with attendants. I had become the wife of Simon, good-natured and penniless fisherman. What did I have to offer my friend?

She shook her head. "I can serve you as I always have."

"No. Take this money and buy your freedom."

"I cannot do that, young mistress. You need money more than before."

"Am I still your mistress?"

"Always."

"Then this is my final command. I wish for your freedom."

"Where would I go?"

"That, my friend, is for you to decide. No one will decide for you again."

Leta lifted her head and looked at me as if for the first time. The gaze that paralleled mine was one of an equal, one of pride. She nodded slowly. Perhaps she would go to Ethiopia, land of her mother's people, where she would be one with a nation that resembled the clearest night skies. Or perhaps she would travel to Alexandria, place of her birth, the bustling heart of civilization and learning. She nodded at me in farewell, her hands grasping the coins. Then she turned down the path, her burden lightened, and disappeared.

———

Our wedding feast was small and meager. Neighbors whispered that I was with child, since we did not wait the year prescribed by the law.

There was no bridal raiment for me or kingly attire for Simon, only fresh flowers which adorned our appearance. My betrothed sported the blossoms of mandrakes in place of a crown, looking a bit like the Greeks' enamored pagan god Bacchus. Daffodils, flamboyant poppies, and irises of ivory and indigo varieties, were woven into an immense garland placed around my neck.

My hair was braided with violet starlike clusters that grow among the rocks along the Galilean shore. Old Salome, the mother of James and John, helped me dress and ensured my complexion was shining with a luster like marble, as the tradition of David prescribed. She was buoyant and talkative, glorying in her role to make me beautiful, as she had no daughter, lending me some gold thread to weave in my dark locks. She even kept a bowl of water in my chamber so I could continually wash my face.

Because I no longer had an ancestral home, Zebedee, the father of James and John, kindly offered his abode to complete the tradition of a bride leaving her father's house to enter her husband's family. I waited for Simon to come for me, to officially welcome me into his tiny home that I had grown to know well. Simon had insisted on honoring tradition, despite our lack of means. None of my family attended, except my mother, who would no doubt suffer a great deal of grief for it. Mother came to give me her blessing, and left quickly, before she would be missed.

Unceremoniously, Simon escorted me back to his home, followed by our few guests Andrew, James, John, and their parents Zebedee and Salome. We had no large processions, no flock of mischievous girls urging me toward my groom. There were no happy children, no music, no dancing. There was only the gregarious chatter of old Salome and the shuffling of Simon's footsteps. I missed the sounds of the lute and drums that accompanied most weddings. Then Simon began whistling as I kept my face veiled and loosed my hair, so the wind tossed my tresses along with violet petals that fell softly as we walked along that short journey from Zebedee's house to Simon's. Our small party carried oil lamps, flickering lights along the darkened streets.

Back at Simon's house, we did have plenty of wine and barley beer; he made sure of that. It was a celebration of marriage, and of new enterprise for ambitious young men. The two other apprentices had left Ephraim's tutelage and joined Simon in a newly formed fishing partnership. Old Salome and Zebedee left the feast early, as he was a slight man with a delicate constitution. Simon,

36

James, and John grew boisterous after prolonged drinking. Andrew grew quieter as his rosy face gave away his inebriation.

"A toast to the youngest fishing team in Capernaum," Simon called, lifting his cup between laughs.

"L'chayim," replied the two sons of Zebedee.

Along with Simon, they gulped down some more beer.

"Our father has agreed to loan us the nets we need," James said.

"Mazel tov!" I could see that Simon was elated.

"It was not I who convinced him." James turned to his brother and patted him on the shoulder. "John was the persuader."

John grinned. "I simply made the case his sons were ready for an independent venture. It was not hard to convince the old man. He remembers what it was like to be young and fearless."

Looking at John, it was difficult to imagine him not being the favorite in any family. He looked young and as comely as a maiden, but he already exceeded Simon in height. His eyes were wide and innocuous, an aquamarine that could darken or lighten according to his mood. James, unlike his younger brother, was a colossus of a man. Tall and broad, he possessed the gargantuan arms of a gladiator. Rivulets of wine hung on his beard and dribbled down his sinewy neck. His mouth was riotously pink, adequately sensuous, and his beard seemed to be something of an obstacle in his face, as he was constantly pulling the unruly mass from his skin. His hair was a wild red at the tips, darkening to rust and then to a sedimentary brown close to his head. The Zebedee brothers were two sides of a coin. John was pale and virtuous while James was robust and gigantic, drinking in the pleasures of life as if there was no tomorrow.

Andrew smiled and held up an empty cup. I rushed to fill it, but he shook his head.

"Brother," Andrew said, "you are neglecting your wife."

All eyes turned to me, still veiled in the betrothal garment. A promised woman was veiled until after the wedding night. Going to the marketplace or collecting water from the well, my face had always been shielded from sight. Even in Simon's home, I wove with the cumbersome film suspended over my eyes. I longed for the night my husband would lift it from my face.

"Ah, yes."

Simon smiled crookedly and drew me to him. He lifted the veil and touched my face; his fingers were cool and calloused. The air felt refreshing to my skin, the first time in weeks. Then he caressed my hair and kissed me lightly on the forehead. I closed my eyes and waited for the kiss to travel to my lips.

"Thank God for an obedient wife!" Simon cried, lifting his cup.

The others responded with raised cups and hearty

congratulations. The drinking resumed; food, fish, and wife were put aside. I sliced open a pomegranate, spouting juice, and I looked back at my husband. My heart fell.

———

Hours later, I ushered the disoriented Zebedee brothers out the door, while Andrew carried Simon up to the roof. He seemed apologetic as he deposited my husband upon the mats, Simon muttering in a confused stupor. I glimpsed up at the stars and clear skies, and I grew even angrier with Simon.

Andrew looked at me with concern. "He only drinks like this when he is happy."

"Thank you, brother. I must attend to my husband." I knew my tone sounded curt, and I regretted it immediately.

I did not see Andrew leave, but I heard his footsteps climbing down the ladder. I pulled off Simon's sandals and moved his legs under the blankets. I removed his mantle and folded it in a pile in a corner. Then I took off my mother's treasured wedding veil and carefully placed in a chest across the room. I looked down at Simon, breathing so peacefully, and I wanted to shake him awake.

Impulsively, I pinched his elbow. He did not stir. I pinched him again.

"I cannot believe you would get drunk on our wedding night," I muttered.

Simon perked up, his eyes bright as he sat up. "I am

not drunk."

My mouth fell open. "What?"

"I am not drunk. But, you, my dear, are exhibiting a tendency for violence." He laughed, feigning pain over his elbows.

"But… but how?"

"If I did not pretend I was drunk, those Zebedee brothers would have forced me to drink until I really was drunk. Then you would have had cause to be angry with me, dear wife."

I offered a small smile. We were silent.

Simon drew me onto the pillows, his mouth covering my mouth, and pressed his body against mine. My husband was patient; he did not rush. I put my hands on his back and melted into his embrace. His lips awakened me to the pleasures of my own body, the pleasures of love, and I groaned. Simon looked deeply into my eyes and held me as I began to feel intoxicated by the sweat and scents of a man. The coarse mats crinkled with our movements and I did not cry out when he took me, as he was gentle. When he entered me again, I did not hold my breath. I began to discover my body as he discovered it, a renewed life that pulsed through both of us.

Afterward, as Simon and I lay still in each other's arms, we traded secrets. Simon told me of his mother's untimely passing and how his father Jonah drank until he died in a tavern brawl a month later. He spoke of his calculating aunt, who raised him out of obligation, and how his cousins bullied Andrew. Simon had run away from Bethsaida seeking work, unskilled though he was. He gathered grains in the fields at harvest and sowed seeds in the spring. He learned to mold the earth with his fingers, but when the farming season ended, he came close to starving. Simon then decided to learn a trade. His fingers were judged too clumsy for carpentry, and he lacked the raw strength for stonecutting. He could not mold clay with his impatient hands, and so found himself dismissed from the potter's charge after a week. As a farmer, he would have been subject to the exploitation of landlords. Simon swore that he would not be a serf to do another's bidding. He sought autonomy, to become his own master. Then he heard that Ephraim was seeking able young men to serve as apprentices. On a whim, he packed his bags, collected Andrew from his aunt's home, and journeyed to Capernaum.

In turn, I told Simon of my longing to see the great caravans of Egypt, and the ancient gods they revered so highly. Even in Galilee, trade routes had grown numerous, and foreign religions proliferated throughout the Roman Empire. I knew of Isis, a goddess who wandered in darkness collecting the remains of Osiris, her husband. I told him of my desire to study in the Great Library of Alexandria, and to hear the story of Gilgamesh the Babylonian in its native tongue.

"To think," my husband said, then chuckled, "Hasar would have taken you to Egypt. Instead, you are stuck with a penniless fellow like me."

"Well," I replied, "at least this penniless putz does not mind that I dream."

Simon pulled the blanket over my head, our arms and legs intertwined like vines. We smothered ourselves in the darkness of our perspiration and kissed each other everywhere. I learned the flavor of Simon's skin, the dampness of his beard before and after coupling, and fell asleep with my hands in his. My husband murmured to me, words lost in the language between dreams and waking.

It was the cold that awakened me. It had only been several hours, yet I had already grown accustomed to the warmth of Simon's body on my bare skin—and missed it when absent. The gray morning light had not yet filtered through the roof, and the fog had begun to rise from the lake, obscuring the resplendent moon. Beside me, the mat was empty and blankets had been carelessly discarded, as if my husband had left in a hurry. Simon's tunics and sandals had disappeared. I blinked, sure that I was dreaming, and tried to shake myself out of the inevitable stupor of waking. As I lit the lamp, a few drops of oil inadvertently landed on my mantle. In the soft glow of the lantern, I looked around. My husband was nowhere to be seen. The ladder leading to the lower quarters of the house was lopsided, even though Andrew had straightened it before descending the previous evening.

I climbed down with lantern in hand, careful to avoid

creaking rungs, as I could hear Andrew's heavy snoring. The oil lamp below glinted from the nail in the wall. I soon found the front door unbolted and slightly ajar. The wind chilled me from within, and ice traveled in my veins. I ventured out with my lantern and its flickering flame, seeking my husband. Tones of saffron and azure painted corners of the dark sky, heralds of the sun. The lake lapped upon the beach, and the sand seemed as ash. Soon, I could see a shadowy figure moving along the dock, pushing a boat out to sea.

"Simon?" I called, running to the dock. Our smaller boat was missing. "Simon!"

The figure did not turn his head and now rowed against the tide alongside a thickening mist that covered Lake Gennesaret, white and nebulous and impervious to the rising sun. He kept rowing until he became engulfed by the impenetrable mist, and it seemed as if the shadowy figure on the lake's surface never existed. Without thinking, I climbed into one of the Zebedee brothers' smaller boats moored to the dock, and began rowing after my husband. There was no storm to fear. I heard the noise of the oars scraping against the sides of the boat, and the bubbling, rippling of water as I struggled to go faster. My muscles tightened as I passed into the mist, and I could see no farther than the tip of the oars and the stern. Even the lantern light was suppressed into a vague glow, resting on the simple plank along the stern.

"Simon?"

Still no response. All around me hung airy columns of mist. I began to hear my own breathing, ragged and uneven. My arms grew tired and I stopped rowing. My boat drifted with the current, taking me where it may. Soft, lustrous tendrils of mist closed over me, and I wondered if I was dying. Then I heard it, the swishing of oars in close proximity. I summoned all my strength into my fatigued arms and rowed toward the sound. Each circular motion felt as if it was tearing my cartilage, bone, and tissue. *Simon, Simon, Simon!* I knew I was moving toward my husband, but whether backward or forward, toward land or farther out into the lake, I did not know.

I was still rowing when the boat hit the grainy shore with a rough halt. I saw Simon's boat, drifting in the shallow waters, unanchored. The sun had risen, filtering through shafts of mist that had begun to dissipate. I saw that we had ended up a good distance down shore from the dock. And then I saw him. Simon lay in a crumpled heap on the beach, face down in the sand. I stumbled to my husband's side and shook him. He moaned and rolled over, swatting at me as if I was a petulant gnat disturbing his reverie. Rivulets of water were on his skin, his eyes were closed, and it appeared he was still asleep. I slapped his arm and he stirred, lifting his elbow protectively over his eyes.

"What… what happened?" he said. He sounded genuinely confused.

"Simon! You risked your life by rowing into the lake

when the mist was thick and impassable. You did not answer me when I called."

I felt exasperation shrouding my soul. All fishermen knew not to go out fishing on a misty morning; this was the kind of mist in which even fish lose their way. I rubbed my hands together, wincing at the fresh blisters from the morning's exertion.

Understanding dawned on Simon as he surveyed us both, drenched and quivering at the crack of dawn. He took me into his bosom, a guilty look upon his face.

When he spoke, his voice sounded as hollow as the cedar planking of our boat: "I walk in my sleep."

I could only stare at him in reply.

He nodded. "I have had this strange habit since my adolescent years, and it occurs only ocassionally, so sometimes I forget that it can happen. I have done it again this night. I had a dream. A voice called me out to the sea. It seemed to come from the sky, a celestial majesty, and yet it felt as familiar to me as my own heart. I had to follow. Then I was running through the house, to the dock, and into the small boat. I rowed into an invisible space on the lake. A storm began to rage around me, columns of water that opened their mouths to receive me. My heart began to pound and I grew afraid. The voice urged me to have faith, to cross into the storm and to emerge unscathed on the other side. 'There is a paradise on the other side of the storm. Follow me.'"

He looked at me, and I gave a slow nod, wanting him

45

to continue.

"But I could not follow," he said. "Rain pelted me like arrows. I began to sink. I saw my hands in the silver glimpses of lightning. I needed to move, to choose a path quickly, or I would drown. I thought of you, the fishing community, Andrew, and my aspirations to build. My heart trembled and I turned back. As I rowed toward the shore and home, I had a sinking feeling that I had chosen unwisely. That I had failed."

Simon stopped and put his head in his hands, rocking back and forth. I was afraid to break the silence. Instead, I sat down beside him and the morning's heat baked our clothes until they felt crisp and dry, although still caked with sand. I could hear insects stutter, and seagulls wrestling for fish. They were the natural fishers, equipped with flight and hooks. A pelican squawked at us, striding along a territory of rocks. My skin prickled with the changing warmth of the hours. Simon just sat there for a long time while the mist dissolved and the sky became a strip of turquoise. Beads of perspiration formed along his temples. He stayed there until Andrew came hiking down the shoreline, looking for him. John and James were about to start fishing for the morning, Andrew said, and they wanted to know the explanation for Simon's interminable delay—and their missing boat.

At Andrew's direct approach, Simon laughed and pulled himself together. "Well, the day must go on, must it not? I was enjoying the sunrise with my new bride.

Women…" He shook his head mischievously, and both men trotted back to the dock.

I sat alone, contemplating the sea, waves foaming into feathers that scattered on the shore. I listened to the waves, whispering secrets in their wisdom and imbibed their lessons. Indeed, such was the plight of women for centuries. I was not immune, and my husband was no exception. Women were the scabs, bloody crusts shielding our husbands' wounds from the world's scrutiny. When the men healed, we fell away without a trace.

We never spoke about the dream again, but I knew it haunted Simon. I learned that my husband was restless, and even his dreams were restless. Always he yearned to gain the admiration of his neighbors, to be a great man. To be ordinary was Simon's greatest fear.

––––––

Our first year was hard. Simon did not have an innate talent for commerce, and his leadership of the fishing company did not go undisputed. Payments to my father Ephraim nearly crippled my husband's fledgling business. Impatient to expand, Simon invested too much in building a second boat and acquiring hooks, nets, and sails. He also insisted on calculating sums and balancing expenditures himself, although Andrew was by far the better bookkeeper. Our debts began to mount. Then came the quarrels with the Zebedee brothers. John proposed to leverage his father's equipment and hire fisherman, since

Simon required more men to man the second boat. That way, John explained, they could maximize the potential of each boat and double their catch every day. Andrew and James heartily favored the suggestion, but Simon balked at the insinuation of accepting charity. "Not charity," James said, "but partnership." Simon shook his head with the obstinacy of a mule, and the frustrated Zebedee brothers stormed back to their father's home.

I heard little of that frustration from my husband, save for the thundering voices that drifted like smoke toward the roof where I wove day after day. Simon never raised his voice with me, never uttered a sharp word. He did not share with me any of the heated discussions of business, which he believed belonged outside of the household.

Andrew finally appealed to me to placate my husband, to soften his resolve without stiffening his pride—Andrew, my confidante, who seldom asked favors for himself and whom I had grown to love more than my own blood brothers. We shared Simon's roof and he remained an encouraging shadow at his brother's side—even when Simon committed the gravest of errors. If Simon was the flame, then Andrew was the torch, anchoring him. It was Andrew who implored me to sway Simon. It was Andrew who reminded me of my power, the ancient powers of influence a wife has over her husband, the way the wind directs the sails of a boat.

Andrew stood on the other side of the loom,

horizontal shafts of wood entwined with rows of wool, running lengthwise from floor to ceiling. Warp threads were held taut by clay weights, and unwoven filaments allowed the light to shine through infinitesimal spaces. As I wove, Andrew's face appeared as an elliptical pattern moving through the loom and I marveled at his wisdom. In that moment, I wondered why he had not married, so keen was his understanding of the relations between man and woman.

Finally, after hearing his heartfelt plea, I knotted the thread and paused before I answered him: "I have never changed my husband's opinion, particularly about his livelihood."

"It must not appear as if you have changed his mind. You would merely… prompt him to consider other matters. Simon must believe that *he* made the decision." His gray eyes, so like Simon's, looked serious.

I raised an eyebrow.

He went on. "My brother seeks to please you, as do all husbands in their intimacy with their wives. However, as Adam was created first, man's ego, particularly one as high and mighty as Simon's, must be preserved."

"Why could you and James and John not persuade him?"

He gave a small shrug. "We lack the gentleness of a woman. In a battle of wills, Simon will never surrender."

I nodded. Andrew rewarded me with a shy smile.

———

I wove as I waited for the appropriate moment with Simon. I thought of the flax I must harvest before summer ended, and then dry on the flat roof for many days before it became suitable for weaving in the month of Elul. Wool, unlike flax, was shorn from sheep and goats in early spring, during the months of Tammuz and Az. Then the fleece was washed, dried, and carded into yarn using a hand spindle. I bartered for woolen yarn from the shepherd's daughter in exchange for fish, and the raw wool felt both soft and prickly in my hands. Whenever I wove wool, I dreamt of the finished masterpiece and orchestrated tones of dye in my mind. Despite the coarser texture of wool, I preferred it to flax because it seemed more alive, containing the temper of sheep, and I could manifest its spirit in the colors I chose. During our barter exchange, I asked the shepherd's daughter if the days were rainy or sunlit, if the flock ran away, and if there were more rams or ewes in the flock. Then I would know to use blue from wood, or yellow from pomegranate. If it was particularly fine wool, I would use the shade made from crushed shells of mollusks, even though that would cost me more than a day's wages. Such were the decisions I liked to make.

Simon and Andrew returned late one evening, long after sunset. I noted that John and James did not accompany them to our table, as had been the custom of recent months. It was just as well, since our meals had grown progressively thinner and more watery. I boiled anchovies in water, but the soup was far too diluted to taste the fish. Our fires had grown smaller to conserve charcoal, butnone seemed to shiver but me. Simon seemed pensive, and his usual gregarious chatter with Andrew was subdued. The younger brother enumerated the mast, sails, and oars requiring repair and the discrepancy between planned and actual expenditures. Then he reminded Simon of Herod Antipas's new decree increasing civilian tribute in the regions of Judea, Samaria, and Galilee. My husband cringed and buried his face in his hands, waving at Andrew to cease. Andrew looked hard at me and then rolled up the papyrus upon which he recorded figures. I served Simon barley beer and offered Andrew water, knowing that Andrew only drank during celebrations, while beer was a daily staple for my husband.

I waited until nighttime, when Simon and I could talk freely. I removed my head cloth and combed my hair, tangled thickets at my waist. I fought my tresses with fierce strokes, and it refused to disengage, so I pulled hard. I was surprised by what the comb yielded: my hair was only a hint of the dark henna that I remembered. Instead, the locks in my lap looked closer to the color of wheat. I thought about the hours I spent weaving on the roof, sitting in the sun. When I lived with my father, my mother had prized her fair complexion, keeping herself and me away from the sun's deteriorating rays.

With that thought, my hands went to my face,

searching for wrinkles. I wondered how else I had changed.

I heard Simon's footsteps ascending the ladder. I began to undress slowly, acclimated to my husband's quiet perusal while I donned nightclothes, and then slipped onto the blankets to look up at him. And Simon had seen me: an amorous look crossed his face. In his penetrating gaze, I was already naked. I began to lift the hem of my tunic, but my husband's hunger would not wait. He tasted me with his lips and his body before I was ready to offer myself. I felt a bit of pain, and something like pleasure too; it seemed lovemaking would be bland without one or the other.

I waited until he lay satisfied and spent beside me, then I spoke. "I have not seen John or James at our table."

Simon snorted. "Those sons of Zebedee have no pride, no sense of independence. They want to engage their father's help to offset our losses. Bah…let them go back to Zebedee. Hardship glorifies success, and if we must suffer in the present time, so be it."

"How long would that be?"

"I cannot tell at the moment."

"This 'help' that John and James speak of, what does it entail?" I treaded gingerly around the words.

"Borrowing labor from among Zebedee's hired men. Zebedee would pay their wages, and they would work for us, manning the second boat."

"Quite generous of Zebedee."

"Indeed. However, I am Simon, son of Jonah, and I will not accept charity from a fellow fisherman. Word travels fast, and your father Ephraim would think us lower than the dust."

"Mm. And so what would make it charity?" I looked into my husband's eyes and tousled his hair.

"We cannot afford to repay him."

"You will in time. Then it will not be charity, merely a prolonged debt. In Capernaum, it is common practice for one businessman to be indebted to another, as long as there is a covenant for repayment."

My husband wore an inscrutable expression on his face.

I decided to tread a little further. "Besides, we have already borrowed nets from Zebedee, and you are partners with his sons. Partnership with the father is a natural step."

Now he shook his head. "I will not be subjugated by another man again. I want to be my own master."

I grinned. I saw it spread across the corners of my mouth, mirrored in Simon's eyes.

"You are your own master, and Zebedee is a good man, respected by the fishing community. Besides, think of the greater bargaining power you will have in collectively bidding for fishing licenses, and contracting with merchants and fish transporters." I lowered my head, and placed my hand on his. "Only a suggestion, my husband. Of course, you know best."

Simon held me by the shoulders, then kissed me with long, hard passion. When I pulled away for breath, he laughed.

"You should be running this fishing enterprise."

CHAPTER III

Despite the best efforts of Simon, Andrew, and the sons of Zebedee, the ensuing winter was one that required perseverance. I began weaving flax for sail linen, which I sold for a small sum in Capernaum and the nearby fishing villages of Bethsaida, Magdala, Tyre, and Sidon. Simon began negotiating marketplace deals with fish merchants, processors, and distributors, while Andrew assumed full bookkeeping responsibilities. John and James directed the labor force of hired men, assessed productivity, and supply needs. While our revenues doubled, my father Ephraim consistently demanded his share, while heavy taxation from Rome and Herod Antipas reduced our earnings to the subsistence level. Herod Antipas, tetrarch of Galilee, was constructing a city in honor of Emperor Tiberius on the southwestern bank of Lake Gennesaret. Herod's vision was to build a metropolis unrivaled in splendor, ordering white marble from Parthia, architects to design aqueducts, and the finest artisans to sculpt the temples. He left the financing of the city Tiberias to his subjects.

Some of our neighbors gave up civilian life and disappeared. Young strapping boys left their farms and fisheries, workshops and forges, taking to the mountains.

It was not uncommon to happen upon an empty cottage or abandoned stall in the marketplace. We felt their absence most in the burden of taxes, redistributed to collect more from those who remained. Herod's taxes and Roman taxes became indistinguishable. Another census might be coming. Rumors of a revolution were brewing: Judas the Galilean was recruiting.

Judas the Galilean was the ghost on the lips of Capernaum men—the new religion. He was a man of unknown origin, except that he hailed from Galilee. Few had met the man, but his myriad aliases became the stuff of legends. Hero. Leader of the Roman Insurrection. Rebel against unjust taxation. Beacon of hope, resisting oppression. He inspired Jewish men to take up arms, to fight. He built a rebel army, and his followers had sprouted like weeds, the fervor in their hearts burning. Zeal, they called it. Righteous indignation over injustice. They called themselves "Zealots." Warriors for the New Jerusalem. Several of my husband's childhood friends, including Simeon the potter, were known to have joined the Zealots.

Over the course of a year of marriage, I learned of an underbelly to my husband's existence as a fisherman. A restlessness. A longing for importance. Simon the Patriot. Simon the Revolutionary. Simon the War Hero. Many times my husband spoke of joining the Zealots. He may even have dabbled in clandestine meetings before we were wed. I only knew him to talk about these affairs, yet even just the talk startled me. The zeal was contagious, engulfing the senses of even the least patriotic of Jews. Revolutionary talk brought an eccentric glint to Simon's eye.

Tongue loosened by wine, Simon recited the litany of taxes and expenses imposed upon common folk: harbor tax, toll tax, tax for road usage, annual Roman tribute, lumber tax, poll tax, custom duties at the gate of each town, fishing and farming leases, rent collection, taxes collected in fish, salt, figs, wine, oil, one-third of grain produce, one-half of produce from fruit and nut trees. The hierarchy of tax collectors, landowning families, Herod Antipas, Emperor Tiberius himself, all took exaggerated measures. The question of survival, or rather, its impossibility, was on the table.

James banged his fists on the table. "Last week, Ananias the farmer hung himself because he could not pay his taxes."

Simon nodded and said, "The Roman Empire is a parasite feeding on the labors of our people."

"We are descendants of Abraham, the chosen people of God. Why must we be subjugated by Rome?" John asked the rhetorical question.

"Because we are not unified," Andrew replied. "How often have we been ridiculed in Jerusalem for our Galilean accent? Or been refused hospitality as we passed through Samaria? Even among our people, Samaritans, Galileans, and Judeans cannot agree."

"Judas the Galilean is our hope," Simon said. "I hear his men number in the thousands. Nearly twenty men in our village alone have left to follow him. He could unify the people."

Andrew looked at his brother. "Casualties of the war are high, Simon. So many of our brothers from this village—Eleazar and Joor and Simeon—have been killed. Their families are afraid to search for their bodies, or even prepare funeral proceedings for them."

"Freedom is borne in blood!" James cried. "The rebels have won great victories in the past three years. They have driven the Romans out of the city of Sepphoris, as well as the surrounding regions of Judea and Galilee."

"There are heavier losses for Judas of Galilee and his followers." The sadness in Andrew's eyes was palpable.

"Make no mistake, the Romans are regrouping," John said. "They will not take defeat lightly. Tiberius will crush the rebellion as an elephant crushes ants. There is talk that the legions of Varus, governor of Syria, are advancing."

———

Rumors of the approaching Roman legions precipitated without any detail. Then without warning, they appeared bearing the insignia of war, the initials SPQR (Senātus Populusque Rōmānus) among their banners, newly polished breastplates, and merciless swords. The soldiers looted the villages and searched every house. No evidence was needed for them to arrest suspects and execute them.

Women fled the streets for fear of rape. Simon forbade me to go to the marketplace and instructed me to hide on the roof. He had heard more than one story of his neighbors' wives catching a soldier's eye. Throughout the regions of Galilee, the Romans' path was marked by crosses, to which Judas's men had been nailed by their wrists and feet, their bones broken with hammers to hasten their death.

The Romans passed through Capernaum in a matter of days, leaving a whirlwind of debris. The marketplace was littered with shards of broken pottery; wheat fields were trampled; fig and olive trees were picked bare of their fruit. Shepherds reported heavy losses in flocks; choicest calves were slain and feasted upon by the Roman interlopers. Houses were burned, and homeless widows roamed the streets, lost in unintelligible mutterings. Children of executed men played with their fathers' tools, awaiting their return. I heard that the rich houses were spared, my father and Hasar no doubt offering the Roman commanders handsome bribes.

I walked to the well with an earthen jug, praying the water would nourish my husband's body, if not his spirit. After the Romans left, Simon was dejected, fearing the worst for Judas the Galilean. He lost his appetite and grew wan, his tangled beard overpowering his face like a wild forest. All his hopes seemed to be extinguished, as the great revolutionary hero seemed destined to die. Each passing day, he waited eagerly for news and rejoiced at the intensified attacks of the rebel army. When he heard of the bloodshed suffered by Judas's men, he sank further into drink. Simon knew the end was inevitable.

A crowd of women had convened at the well, many in mourning robes. They poured water into jugs and jars, and over their faces to wash away the sorrow. Rebellion had seeped into the heart of Capernaum. "Oh my son, my son!"—strapping boys on the verge of manhood, leaving their bones to their mothers. I peered into the bucket and to my relief, the water was clean. My jug full and resting its cool clay surface against my breast, I turned to leave.

"Water! Water! Water!"

It was a cry of desperation. A large man hobbled to the well. His face was partially covered by his red mantle, but his lips were visible, parched and cracked with fever. His sunburned hands gripped a cane that he used as a third leg. Faltering, he caught himself with great effort and pushed forward by sheer will. He leaned his tremulous body against the cistern, kneeling as bloody leg injuries deprived him of his natural height. He repeated his supplication, and his accent revealed him to be a native Galilean.

No one spoke. The women involuntarily shrank back after catching their breaths. The stranger stank. He gave off medicinal odors—wine and oils used to heal wounds. His mantle, however, smelled of sweat, urine, and excrement. Heat emanated from his body. I was closest to the well, so I dipped my cup into the water and handed it to the man. He drank deeply, water dribbling down his chin and throat, but he did not seem to notice. His skin was so dry and cracked that I knew he had been starving. Yet the proud lift of his chin intimated that this man was no beggar.

As I turned to depart again, he pulled me by the sleeve and his grip felt deathlike. "I am seeking the dwelling of Simon, son of Jonah."

"What business have you with my husband?"

"I bear him vital news."

I felt startled. I did not know what to do, but his tone sounded so insistent that I relented. I wrenched away from his hold, ripping my tunic in the process.

"Come, I will take you there."

I walked slowly so that he could follow me. We walked away from the rolling hills of the market square toward the footpaths of the fishing community, which was at a significantly lower elevation. At the steep decline, the man struggled to breathe, and when I offered myself as a crutch, he did not refuse. His stink was nauseating, and I covered my mouth with my mantle. As we approached the Sea of Galilee, he leaned completely on me, unconscious. His weight felt enormous, and I simply could not take the next several steps to our house. A curved dagger brushed my side, and I leaped back, startled. Most fishermen and village men were unarmed, and did not conceal weapons this way. He must have been a soldier. My water jug shattered. The stranger tumbled into the sand, and his mantle fell away from his face revealing a wound from a shard of pottery.

I gasped.

Blood gushed from a gash extending from forehead to mid-cheek, between his right eye and the crooked ridge of his nose. His right nostril was split open, spouting blood that crusted the right side of his face. I hurriedly wiped his face with my mantle, and wished I had not spilled the water so I could wash his face. I began to bandage his nose with my head scarf.

"What is this? What has delayed you?"

Simon had come up from behind me, his hands situated on his hips.

"This poor man has been seeking you. For pity of God, his wounds are severe."

My husband was staring at the fallen man, horrified at what he saw.

"I need to fetch the rapha." I got up to my feet.

Simon grabbed my arm with such urgency that he bruised my wrist. His voice was grave: "Woman, alert no one. This is Simeon the potter. We grew up together. He disappeared years ago to follow Judas the Galilean."

CHAPTER IV

"Taxes!" Simeon the potter cried woefully. Half delirious, he ranted into the night. I feared his ramblings would wake the neighbors, some of them poor enough to seek reward from Roman authorities. While none would ever admit to betraying a Galilean to foreigners, these were desperate times, and the Romans were cunning in granting anonymity to informers.

He needed to be watched, and we all kept vigil at Simeon's side. Andrew had given up his mat, and I slept by the fireplace to tend to the potter's wounds. His legs looked like they might be saved, as the flesh was muscular and the bone was strong. Despite his injuries, blood loss was minimal. The face, though hideous, would heal. The culprit we feared most was the fever. I changed cloths soaked in cold water hourly and laid them on his forehead, but to no avail. I knew no other remedies for fever. The rapha once told me that fevers were a warning, before the body lost the instinct to live. I feared he was dying.

We waited. We prayed that Simeon's youth and strength could overcome this affliction. *Lord, we deliver Simeon the potter into your all-powerful hands, so you may restore him.* Simon wrung his hands in anguish, hungry for news. Andrew sat beside him, contemplating a ledger. I kept the fire roaring and placed more mats on the unconscious potter, hoping to make him sweat. Despite the heat, I felt cold and my skin tingled. I glanced at Simeon's bloody garments strewn on the floor, wondering how many were like him, dying while families awaited their return. The war had touched us finally, and wars leave no one unscathed.

I fell asleep on the table, my neck stiff as the ancient wood. I opened my eyes to Andrew holding a bowl of cool water for the potter to drink. Simon hovered beside him impatiently. The potter sat up, his eyes bright and alert, despite the bruising of his face. He held his hand hesitantly to his nose, startled at the damage, and then withdrew his fingers quickly.

"I thought I had dreamt it."

Looking downward, Simon shook his head. "We are losing the war."

It was not a question, and there was no need for Simeon to answer.

"How bad is it?" Simon asked.

"The Romans are closing in on us. They launched a double-pronged attack, breaking our retreat by the river Jordan and moving northward at Jericho." The potter's voice sounded so weary. "Varus led another legion from the north, blocking our survival lines. There are so many of them."

"Where are they now?" Andrew asked.

"Sepphoris. The wounded are in an old storehouse, used as headquarters. You must go there." Simeon then cocked his head toward the fisherman brothers.

The shock that must have registered on my face was mirrored by both sons of Jonah. My husband took a step back.

"Simon," Simeon said. "We grew up like brothers. Our homes were side by side in the village. I saved you from drowning once. I have never asked anything of you. Please. You must find Judas."

My husband's silence emboldened the potter to continue: "I would give my life for him, but it is not enough. Judas is terribly injured, maybe dying. Without him, there is no hope. Without him, the war is lost."

"The war is already lost," Andrew said quietly. "We are fishermen, not soldiers."

Simeon eyed him. "I am not asking you to kill, but to save."

"You are asking us to fight," Andrew said.

"You are asking them to die!" I knew it was not my place, but still I spoke. I gripped my husband's hand and said, "If you are caught, you will be executed with the rest of the rebel army."

Simon pulled away and glowered at me. "This is for men to decide."

I sat down, my cheeks hot with embarrassment.

Andrew looked at his brother. "Your decision affects the family, and it is best made by the entire family.

Romans are everywhere. It is a huge risk."

"Freedom is not won without cost," Simeon said. "If you hesitate, Judas will die waiting. Please, my friend. You hold the destiny of Israel in your hands."

Simon began to pace.

The potter watched him, then said, "Simon, this is your time to fight. The revolution needs you. There are no more men to save him. Most of us have been crushed by the Romans, dead or broken, like me. The army has scattered. This is your chance to be a hero. Show me you are not all talk. Show me you are not a coward. Show me you are a man."

Simon stopped. The silence felt so thick, one could cut through it with a knife. The potter waited for his words to take the desired effect.

Finally, Simon said, "I will go to Sepphoris."

Andrew stepped forward. "Brother—"

Simon held up his hand. "I have decided. Will you come, Andrew?"

Andrew grimaced, then nodded. "This is for you, Simon. Not this senseless war."

———

So began my time of waiting. Sepphoris was a three-day journey from Capernaum, and the brothers wasted no time preparing for their laborious task, complete with a donkey for the wounded Judas. I bade Simon good-bye, then pursed my lips and eyed the young donkey trotting beside them, tail flailing from side to side. Neither fisherman wanted to ride, preferring to keep it fresh for the delicate load on the way back.

The Romans were reinforcing regiments in this region of Galilee, around the city of Sepphoris and surrounding villages: Bethlehem, Nazareth, Bethsaida, and Capernaum. I knew the massacre had not ended, and the cruelty of Roman legionaries had reached far and wide among conquered peoples. Twenty years ago, a massacre of children had taken place in Bethlehem, ordered by Herod the Great and executed by Roman soldiers. Children under the age of three were slaughtered without sense, rhyme, or reason. The wailing of heartbroken parents echoed for years, catching the attention of my mother, who had traveled to visit the tomb of Rachel during a religious festival. She had met a woman who never recovered, carrying a threadbare swaddling cloth that she held against her cheek, whispering, "Elijah."

I continued to attend to Simeon the potter, bandaging his injuries and serving food as befitting a guest. He did not expect me to speak and I did not intend to. He seemed a ghost in my house. I wove my days away, and also conversed with John and James at the fishing dock. I had told them my husband and his brother had been called away on an urgent family matter in Bethsaida, which they accepted without the slightest doubt.

I began to notice a change in my body, and a persistent illness that resulted in vomiting. Usually, it came in the mornings, but sometimes also in afternoons when I was weaving. The smell of fish began to rouse waves of nausea in me, and I began to have unusual cravings: pomegranates at midnight, olives in mid-morning. Not until I did not bleed that month did I know for sure.

One evening, after Simon's departure, there came an insistent rapping on the door. I knew by the strong, measured hand who was beyond the threshold.

It was Levi the tax collector.

Towering like a young cypress tree, the publican scrutinized me. He was dark of cheek and brow, shaven as a Roman, with an angular jaw. The smell of dusk washed inside—bruised fruit, unsold fish, and disobedient animals… disappointments of the day.

"Shalom, Master Levi." I bowed my head slightly.

"Shalom." He leaned on the frame of the doorway. "On behalf of the Roman Empire and Herod Antipas, your quarterly taxes are due. I also need to evaluate your assets."

I barred his entry with my arm. "Our assets are at the fishing dock," I said.

The publican craned his neck and took a step forward. A small scar below his temple became visible—from a scuffle with Simon years ago.

"This property is considered an asset, and it is my responsibility to determine its worth for taxation purposes."

I felt my chest tighten. "My husband is not home. These matters are best settled by men."

"It is not necessary for your husband to be present while I perform my duties. Make way, woman."

Levi pushed his way through as if I was less than wind; his strides wide and formidable. No wonder windows were closed and locks fastened wherever he passed.

"No… no!" I said. "I… I have not cleaned to my satisfaction. It is not ready."

He narrowed his eyes and entered Andrew's living quarters, where Simeon the potter reclined on the mat, eyes half-open.

"Who is this?" Levi asked.

I froze, unable to utter a word. *I had betrayed Simon, Andrew… all of us.*

"Answer me, woman!"

"It is I, Simeon the potter. Do you not recognize me?"

Levi's mouth fell open. "So… the rumors are true: you have become a Zealot."

Simeon stared up at him. "Go on… take me. Claim your reward. Do not implicate Simon and his wife. They are innocent."

Levi cast a glare in my direction. "Harboring fugitives is a crime. You are all guilty. You will be judged by the law."

"What law?" Simeon said. "There is no law. Only Roman greed. You tax collectors lap it up—subservient dogs!"

Levi's eyes grew wide and he raised his voice: "It is you criminals that give our people a bad name! You have made it impossible for the Romans to trust the Jews!"

"Jew?" Simeon snorted. "You still think yourself a Jew?"

Levi had once been considered a Jew. Son of Alphaeus and a Seleucidite woman, he was a promising young scholar and excelled in languages, particularly Greek, Latin, and Aramaic. In accordance with his namesake, Levi was prepared to enter the synagogue and study to become a rabbi. It was believed that his Syrian blood tainted him, leading him astray. Villagers whispered that he was shameless, a traitor—how could he extort money from his own people?

Simeon's insult cut the publican deeply. He pulled his dagger from his tunic and brought it to the potter's throat. Simeon made no move to resist. At the same time, Levi grabbed me by the waist with his other hand, his thick rings cutting through the thin linen of my tunic. I did not have the will to resist.

"You are both going to the Roman garrison. You will be charged with sedition."

"Please!" I cried.

I fell to my knees. I looked up at Levi the publican, garbed in his rich saffron robes and fine leather sandals, appearing distressed and conflicted.

"Show us mercy," I said. "Simon, I, and Simeon—we

are your people. We share blood from the same forefathers. The Romans will never consider you kin. We are one people; that can never change, no matter what your profession."

The tax collector hesitated.

I went on. "Do you not have a mother? A wife? Spare us. Please. For the sake of a woman who loves her husband. For the sake of an unborn child."

Levi swallowed. He did not answer, but I saw the struggle in his eyes, the wavering of his adamantine methods and the flickering of a new beginning. Then he loosened his grip. Simeon the potter slumped back onto the flurry of mats and blankets.

The publican turned his head toward the door. "You were never home. I did not call on you today."

————

Simon and Andrew returned several weeks later, haggard and demoralized. Their faces looked shrunken from rapid weight loss, their clothes caked with dried mud. Andrew's cheeks were scratched. They seemed to have walked out of hell.

"What happened?" I said. "Why are you—"

Simon shook his head dejectedly. Andrew appeared dazed, seeing Simeon and me peripherally as his eyes focused on some distant apparition.

The potter watched both fishermen. He kept glancing behind them, awaiting a third arrival. When it was clear that the sons of Jonah had returned alone, Simeon paled and shuddered.

"Where is Judas?" The voice came as barely a squeak.

My husband looked so broken that I longed to cradle him to my breast. However, I knew better than to move in the company of a guest. I kept my station.

Simon kept his eyes fixed on the floor. "We were too late."

Simeon shifted onto his back, no longer having the strength to hold himself upright.

My husband continued to speak, his voice wavering: "The road to Sepphoris was long and tortuous. Men were hanging on crosses, some dead, some dying, wishing for a swifter end. The legionaries were methodical: all crossbars were identically assembled; victims were stretched out like papyrus drying in the sun. Every ten paces. There was little blood, only open wounds where nails were driven into the wrists and feet. Legs were bent sideways, thin shinbones already broken and more crooked than the legs of puppets. They were stripped of every thread, exposed like animals. The executions were fresh, and we could hear the whimpering of those still alive."

Simon paused and drew in a heavy breath before continuing. "Andrew stopped and wept bitterly for the wrongs endured by our countrymen. 'Where is God to allow this suffering?' he asked. I did not know how to answer; I kept walking. The city of Sepphoris was destroyed by fire. Survivors were scattered, poking through charred remains of their homes before they bundled their salvaged possessions and headed south to Jericho or Jerusalem. Gone was the majesty of marble, the metropolis boasting of Greek culture and bustling commerce. Nothing but ashes.

"As we diverged from the main road, a handful of relatives arrived to take down the bodies. We started toward them to offer assistance, but the soldiers' watchful eye fell upon us. They were looking for semblances of disorderly conduct, to arrest the remaining rebels. We could only watch as old women and children looked about for good souls to aid them, but seeing none, they wrestled down the bodies with difficulty. Then the mourning began, plaintive voices blending into one sad song. Andrew counted the crucified men lining the roads, numbering seventy-three."

As Simon paused again, my breath caught.

"We traveled onward to the storehouse, and the sun began to sink behind the mountains as we entered. It had been abandoned for days, but I could see the signs of fighting, dead men littering the ground like tombs of a graveyard, Roman and Jew alike. The earth was upturned in areas for makeshift graves. The smell of decay was profuse, as were final attempts to stifle it—medicinal oils and wines. We flipped the bodies to examine them, futilely searching for Judas. How could we identify him?"

Now Simon looked at me, then at the bedridden potter and continued. "'Who are you?' someone asked. A tall man emerged from the shadows, carrying a long sword blacker than charcoal. His eyes were wells of blue. The angles of his face would be dashing and debonair in times of peace, but he appeared ruthless in the midst of battle. His fury was palpable.

"I said, 'We have come for Judas.'

"'I am he.' We were baffled. His smooth Judean accent was impeccable. He sounded educated, of the gentry perhaps. Surely this healthy warrior was not the wounded Galilean leader we had been sent to save. Andrew was skeptical as well: 'We were told that he is hurt.'

"Judas eyed him and asked, 'Who told you that?'

"I said, 'Simeon the potter of Capernaum. He has fought at Judas's side these three years. We are his neighbors from Capernaum. I am Andrew and this is my brother Simon.'

"The warrior lowered his sword; the mercenary scowl faded from his face. 'So you are not informers,' the man said. He sighed, then stated, 'The leader is dead.'"

I heard the injured potter gasp.

Simon shook his head. "I could not utter a word. Andrew led to me a railing for support. He asked the question I could not bear to ask: 'How did this happen?'

"'I am not certain myself,' the man said. 'I was scouting on the military's movements. I believe they took him with the wounded here.' The warrior drove his sword deep into the ground with rage. 'If he had not sent me to investigate the enemy at the last minute, I would have been by his side! Do you think the Romans could have taken him if I were here? Our brothers never denounced him; that much I know. The Romans themselves are not sure if they had captured Judas the Galilean. They sent more squads here and I cut them down, one by one. They deserved no mercy. Each time I slit a soldier's throat, I eased my vengeance.'

"So how are you sure he is really dead?' Andrew asked.

"'I saw him.' The warrior's eyes sparked an angry, austere blue. 'I saw him hanging on a cross.'

"We had nothing else to say. The man said, 'Go now. The legionaries will return. The Romans always return to bury their dead. I can see you are not men of combat. You will only slow me down.'

"I nodded, then asked, 'Do you need us to bring a message to your family? In Judea?'

"He shook his head. 'I have no family,' he said, 'save brothers of the revolution. I am from Kerioth. My name is also Judas.'

"Despite the dark, we headed back to the roads as thunder rumbled above us. It was heavy, oppressive rain that pelted down upon both the just and unjust. My thoughts felt as dark as the rain: *All is lost. The war is over and Jews remain an overpowered people. Not even a people. We are a collection of tribes, disgruntled and bickering among ourselves, dispersed and powerless as sand. I had believed in the revolution, but now all I see is a terrible waste.*

"Our footsteps were heavy with mud, and we removed our sandals so we would not lose them. Andrew had fallen silent, but he halted his tracks and pointed in the northeastern direction. We saw a squadron of Romans, fully armed and marching in the rain, headed toward the storehouse. They had the look of hunters before a kill. We would be immediate suspects, caught near the site of rebellion. There was no cover on the open road, between here and the storehouse. Within moments, we would be visible, two shabby men lurking in the night. Rain drenched us to the bone, and we instinctively ran back for shelter.

"Judas was nowhere to be seen. It was black as pitch inside the storehouse, as if all light in the world had gone out with a single breath. The darkness was thicker than the rain, and we were at a loss, not knowing where to hide. We were doomed. Outside, the soldiers were fast approaching, their steps rumbling over the rocky hillside. I thought of the corpses around us, alive hours or perhaps days ago; how still they lay now, life and death separated by a tenuous strand. And then it came to me.

"'Andrew! Quick!' I said. 'Lie still near the corpses. Pretend we are dead.' It was cowardly, but I convinced myself at the time it was more imperative to live. Only later did I learn that Andrew had slipped and knocked his head, falling unconscious in the dirt. Minutes later, the door opened slowly and the hinges creaked. I counted six, seven men, who stomped forward, surrounding the area, and one who held a lantern, peering over the bodies and examining faces. Kicking and flipping me over with his foot, I did not breathe and he seemed satisfied. The rain had rendered us cold and wet, and the soldier did not bother checking pulses.

"'They are all dead, sir,' the soldier said.

"'How many are ours?' came the reply.

"'Three.'

"'Prepare to bring them to camp. You four, follow me. We will scout the surrounding territory for any remaining insurgents.'

"'What about the others, sir?'

"'Toss all other dead bodies in a pile at the edge of the city. Rebels were sighted at this location. I want it under surveillance.'"

Here, Simon paused in his recounting of the horror he and Andrew had endured. He closed his eyes and then finally went on. "The commanding officer gave another order, and we were thrown into a cart, pushed back into the devastating open sky. I was crushed between the bodies, their blood and fluids washed by rain as it washed my face. I did not think of them as martyrs so much as foolish men, stubborn and blind to a cause that killed them. *Liberation is not possible in our generation,* I thought. It was a brief journey, but somehow I swallowed the stench of death, their cadaverous flesh next to ours. The Romans unloaded us quickly; no care was taken to preserve the bodies. We were casualties of war. We were not meant to be buried."

Now my husband's voice broke. "Is this the consequence of faith? Whatever happened to the might that diminished David's enemies? Where is the power that stopped the Egyptians from pursuing Moses?" My husband's voice faded and his shoulders slumped.

"Perhaps... God has abandoned us." Andrew spoke without passion. While his face was contorted from earlier weeping, he seemed exhausted, drained of emotion.

I stood there, more horrified at my husband's despair than anything. "Surely you don't believe that of God."

Simon shrugged. "I don't know. Perhaps he likes to amuse himself. Perhaps we petty creatures only serve his pleasure, and he likes to see us squirm."

Simeon the potter raised his fist. "I don't believe in prophecies, oracles, or that God would concern himself with our affairs. I only believe in myself, the might of man."

Then I thought of something: "Where is the donkey?" I asked.

All three men seemed irritated by the question.

Only Andrew bothered to answer: "He was stolen on the second day. Before Sepphoris."

The donkey was the result of a trade from a bolt of wool I had spun. It was my small contribution to cause of Israel, and to the efforts of the men.

I wanted to tell Simon then. I wanted to share the news that made every woman blush with pride. My husband, however, was fatigued and occupied in his own thoughts. Dreams of a son were preceded by dreams of a people and dreams of God.

CHAPTER V

Figs began ripening and almond trees were blossoming when Simeon the potter departed three weeks later. It was the month of Shebat, the season of awakening, and Galilee flourished in dark greens of sprouting vine leaves. The potter bid us farewell and headed to Magdala, where he had relatives, conveniently unaware of his revolutionary past. Andrew's presence in the household became rare; every spare moment was spent questioning elders in the synagogues, divining the meaning of existence and evidences of God. My husband threw himself into fishing as if there was no tomorrow, finding the salty tempests of Gennesaret easier to endure than the storm festering in his soul. I waited and waited for the appropriate moment, but the days went by in a flurry of washing, mending, weaving, and baking bread. Simon was often too tired to talk at night. The knowledge kept me awake in the ambiguous hours before dawn, pushing obstinately as the seed inside me soon would.

Hearing my husband shuffle in one evening, I finally blurted out, "I am carrying your child."

Simon did not stir. The stillness was an absence, a gap in this continuous darkness in which my husband did not reach for me. I did not know whether this news would bring elation or frustration.

"How long have you known?" he finally said.

"One month—the day you returned from Sepphoris."

"Why have you waited to tell me?"

"I was waiting for the right moment."

His arms tightened around me, and his breath tickled my neck. We slept until the cock crowed.

———

The change in Simon was indiscernible at first, like the flowering in my belly. Slowly, I began to notice the differences. My husband did not wake me at dawn, and he crept around in the darkness without a lamp to avoid disturbing my slumber. Simon ate considerably less and spooned the excess into my bowl during mealtimes, much to the amusement of Andrew and the sons of Zebedee. There was the hammering in the evenings, a candle flickering beside him. Simon complained of working in poor light, but he guarded the fruit of his labor with great secrecy. No amount of pleading would sway him.

My belly was slow in thickening; weeks and months would pass before my condition became visible to the neighbors, I knew. I felt certain it was a boy. Only a boy could cause the churning, roiling within me. My insides thundered, and I spent many mornings cleaning the vomit, hurled like a projectile from my mouth. Perhaps this was the stuff of ambition. Then there was the shape of the swelling. The ancients believed that a smooth, round belly denoted a girl, while a pointed belly intimated a boy's battle instincts, even from the womb. My mother had known of my obstinate nature before I was born. I knew from the kicking and nights of cold perspiration that it was a boy.

As the scorching month of Elul softened into the gentler days of Tishrei, Simon announced that he was making me a bed. Limited as he was in his carpentry skills, my husband was unable to make anything but a simple bed. The months he had spent as an apprentice to a carpenter were put to good use and produced adequate, if rudimentary, knowledge. He was able to assemble the larger pieces of wood, but lacked the nuances that only an expert could provide. The end result was a lopsided bed, one end higher than the other, and it creaked. Nevertheless, a creaking bed was better than none; my body ballooned suddenly and became very cumbersome.

―――

In the seventh month of my pregnancy, John and James decided to journey to Jerusalem for the Feast of Tabernacles. Andrew remained ambivalent, unsure about the fidelity of God, but they persuaded him to go with them. Simon thought my condition much too delicate to travel, and declined to journey without me. Besides, someone was needed in Capernaum to oversee the fishing business, as hired laborers were known to cheat masters in their absence.

With his partners gone, my husband grew increasingly busy and I spent much time alone. Along with vacillating hungers for the sweet and bitter, my temper had become inconstant. I growled at Simon and at stubborn flax threads that would not respond to my weaving fingers. I howled if the sun burned like a furnace or heavy rains poured down on my rooftop chamber, leaking onto my bed. I cried if my husband returned late and berated him if he came home before I had finished baking bread. In short, there was no pleasing me.

I was readily irritated at the footsteps climbing the ladder to my room as I sat weaving. Why was Simon home at this hour? It was barely midday, and the sun had not reached its zenith in the sky. I prepared myself to reprimand my husband, how he should be more responsible now that a baby was on the way, that he was too old to yield to the adolescent impulse of leaving whenever he wished.

It was not Simon who appeared at the top of the ladder.

It was my mother.

I had not seen my mother for three years, although I had sent word to her I was with child. Now I stared at her through my loom. Age seemed to have descended upon her suddenly, like the wilting of a rose. Streaks of white had crept into her dark hair, though still long and lustrous. Her skin looked dimpled, and her countenance was a solemn lake. I saw a profound sadness in her eyes.

"Your father is dead."

There were no pleasantries. Years had passed with little contact, and she spoke as she always did, baring the truth. I stared at her, not comprehending what I heard. The world seemed to stop. I heard the turtledoves whistling and the wind murmuring outside my window. I heard the wailing of the seagulls, waves plunging under steadfast rocks and dissipating. The blaring sun ceased to hurt my eyes. Through my loom, I saw threads dividing us, dividing time, and I was on the other side of lost time.

Abba!

I sat for a long while, listening because there was nothing else I could do. I did not notice how the day progressed, my mother moving about the house or my husband coming home. Then I remembered and sprang to my feet. There was work to do. The Law required families to bury our dead within one day, since heat and moisture would spoil the body and damage its ritual purity.

I found my mother downstairs and asked, "Have you prepared him for burial? When is the funeral procession? My condition is rather burdensome, but I can be ready within the hour." I glanced down at my huge belly, bulging despite the loose-fitting mantle that covered my body like a blanket.

My mother shook her head morosely. "Everything is over. Your father has already been buried."

"What? When?"

"Seven days ago."

So even the accepted period of grieving was over. My heart sank.

"Your father gave very specific instructions. Under no circumstances were Simon the fisherman and his wife to be informed before the mourning period had passed. Reuben and Levi threatened the slaves with severe punishments if they disobeyed."

I turned on my husband. "A funeral procession is no small matter. How could you not be aware?" I asked, hearing the sharp tone in my words but not caring.

He sighed, his voice tired. "I have been busy dealing with a labor crisis. I would not know even if Herod Antipas had expired."

My mother put a hand on my arm. "I am sorry, my daughter, but I had to remain faithful to his wishes. I could not deny a dying man his peace."

I frowned, a bitter taste in my mouth. So it was my existence that gave him no peace. In my mind's eye, the mourning procession would have been grandiose, the way Ephraim liked all things. My mother, Levi, and Reuben would have washed my father's body and anointed him with costly oils as well as spikenard. They would have brought a mixture of myrrh and aloes, eighty or a hundred pounds, about half my father's weight. It was the finest linen they would use, woven by my mother's own dexterous fingers. They would have wrapped the spices within folds of linen, draping the burial shroud around his

85

body like a cocoon, pouring lamentations over every fold. When my father was tightly bound in cloth, they would have hired professional criers and mourning women. Along with their own tears, they would have flooded the town with sorrow. Tambourines would have rung, bemoaning Ephraim the fisherman's departure from this world and heralding his journey into heaven.

Abba!

I closed my eyes and raised my head skyward. Something inside of me crumbled and an excruciating pain overtook my body, convulsing in my womb. It was as if an unseen hand reached into the fruit of motherhood, scraping my insides with claws. The seed within me, so firm before, began to wobble. *My son, my son!* The nourishing lake inside of me broke and dribbled down my thighs.

I dreamt that the sky was red. I did not see my father, but I knew he was near. I was searching for his tomb. In accordance with the Law, it was located on a hillside outside of Capernaum. The earth was parched and the air had turned cool in the last days of Kislev. The bedrock wall of the tomb looked forbidding, a gateway to where the flesh of Ephraim's body disintegrated, allowing the soul to resurrect. I came to collect my father's bones.

I unrolled the stone, and dry leaves drifted to my feet, crackling. I saw the white linen wrapping, and the bony form underneath. I carried an ossuary, preparing to place each part of my father in the vessel, the duty of a daughter.

Before I could touch him, the entire body was burning. A bolt of lightning struck the ossuary, shattering it.

"Sacrilege!"

It was my father's voice.

I awoke writing with pain. My mother was shouting frantically and I recognized the grunting of the Mesopotamian midwife. They had eased me onto the bed, my beautiful new bed. My mother stood on my right, squeezing my fingers with a reassuring pressure. The midwife placed bricks beneath my hips and spread my legs apart as if they were wings. Her hands felt gentle and steady, although I did not understand her furious muttering. It seemed an incantation, a chant to ward off evil spirits.

The pangs came and subsided, each wave more agonizing than the next. Sobs broke from my lips and I held onto my mother; she cooed soft encouragements into my ear. Her brow furrowed in worry, and I realized that the midwife also seemed afraid.

I screamed and I wept and I prayed. I vomited and my knees were bent. Why did I not know that my body was to be tested? Why had no one told me that birth is the struggle for survival, and only the strong survive? This was the suffering of women for centuries, Eve and her progeny repenting for sin. Out of sorrow, we would bring forth children.

Then I began to push. I pushed and pushed until I was expelling my senses from my body, but no baby. I longed to empty myself of this rock, to relieve the anguish, or to die. I pushed until I might explode. Time passed. No progress. I began to fear I was not strong enough. The midwife and my mother exchanged glances, the look when the ordinary passage of life onto life became a battle between life and death.

I did not know flesh could rip like cloth.

My son was born, wrinkled and dripping with mucus; all ten fingers and toes intact. He lay so very still. I let out a shriek. The midwife hurriedly cut the cord and attempted to breathe life back into him, to pull his soul from the clutches of death. She rubbed salt on his tiny body to prevent infection.

It was too late.

He did not cough, did not stir. His lips were blue. His hair was thick and brown, eyes sealed shut. They would never open to see the world. They would never see the loving face of his mother or the pride of his father. They would never see the sun, or the moon, or the stars. They would never see Galilee blossom into evanescent greens and soften into resplendent golds. My son had died blind. When had my son died?

And in the heaviness of dark emotion that descended upon me, I began to bleed. Cries of alarm from my mother and the midwife came from far away. I felt life draining from me and I was glad. I wanted to sleep and to forget. I wanted to surrender to the same fate as my son. I fell back upon the pallet and I knew nothing more.

When I awoke again, Simon was beside me, looking more forlorn than when he returned from Sepphoris. The plain beneath his eyes was so dark it seemed smudged with ink. My mother was holding my hands, our fingers interlocked as if we were praying. My head slumped back into the pillows. Why was I still alive?

"I thought I had lost you," Simon whispered, kissing me. "You were unconscious for three days."

"You lost a lot of blood," my mother remarked, changing the wet cloth on my forehead.

"My son," I mumbled through dry lips.

My husband and my mother looked disturbed at the prospect of telling me, but I already knew. A mother knows when she has lost her child. My body began quivering, the wounds fresh and pinning me back into the bed. My breasts were full of milk and heavy, ready to nurse. I broke into a cry.

"My son!"

I wept until I had no tears left. I screamed until it seemed the very earth was screaming. I did not ask about burial, because I knew it had already been done. My son, the son of Simon bar Jonah, had been put into a tomb without a name.

———

Andrew and the sons of Zebedee returned from Jerusalem after two moons, their journey delayed by one month longer than planned. They came at dusk, shaking the dust from their sandals. Andrew was the most joyous, expecting the arrival of our child after his arduous sojourn. He had invited James and John to praise the fertility of his brother's wife and to share in the hospitality of his table. Instead, they were greeted with silence, an emptiness wrought by tragedy, and we had nothing to offer besides bitter herbs and the bread of despair.

Simon had felt the burden of their absence; long days at the fishing dock made him querulous. My mother assumed my domestic responsibilities while I lay in bed without the resolve to live. Small things that had brought me pleasure seemed bland. I drifted into melancholy, in and out of consciousness. Sometimes, I would dream of my son. I would touch his fingertips when he was whisked away by the shadows. I would hear a child's laughter fading into the distance. Every time I came near, he would dissolve. It was a cruel game.

———

The month of Adar brought high winds, and Lake Gennesaret raged in tumultuous storms that swallowed fish and fisherman alike. I longed for the waves to engulf me, burying me in their watery depths. My wounds healed slowly and my fingers resumed weaving, but I was a stranger in my own body. Since the death of my son, I had ceased to speak. Words seemed futile to one who wished to disappear.

My mother was my chief comfort, she who had borne

six children and buried three. She brought me nourishing soups of mandrakes and applied balsam to my scars. She ground the grain and kneaded the dough in my stead, making sweet loaves flavored with oil, mint, cumin, cinnamon, and locusts. She even baked honey cakes by frying them in the pan, and then urged me toward my favorite childhood treat. Alas, I was no longer a child; I had crossed the threshold to womanhood. I brought a baby into this world and I was unable to save him. I had failed.

My mother understood. She whispered tales of her deceased offspring; she had memorized the color of their hair and gave them each a name. She sang songs for them, an eldest boy who died of the plague and twin russet-haired girls who lasted only seven days after their birth. She told me they became angels by the Lord's side, and she could hear the rustling of their velvet wings at night. The fiber of their souls was too pure to be subjected to this world, and God in his pity had called them home to spare them suffering. It was the flawed ones that remained living. It was we who would be judged. The innocents had already tasted the fruits of heaven

I listened to the humming of her voice without responding. My mother did not expect me to answer. She spoke tenderly, reminding me to keep the spirit strong so the body would heal. My mother assumed the tasks of mending, washing, and baking without complaint. Simon certainly did not miss my cooking amid my mother's delectable creations with fish, and she celebrated the return of my strength day by day. She served fish broiled or roasted over a slow fire, minced with olives, stewed with leeks for a tender flavor, fried with egg, or steamed in milk for a delicate and flaky taste. For special occasions, she mixed wine with fish brine for a poignant sauce served with bread.

Simon was patient with me, although I knew that he felt equally crushed by the loss of our son. "Bar-Simon," he mumbled in his sleep as I lay in his embrace, waiting for the darkness to end. Simon slumbered heavily, but the nights were intolerable for me. When my eyes closed, I saw the silhouette of my child with his face turned away. He was sinking into the ubiquitous shadows. I was running, chasing him, but I could not stop him from drowning in the tormented black sea. Then he was gone. I was alone, shrieking his name, the name that my husband had bestowed upon him without my knowledge. *Bar-Simon.*

My husband held me close, as if he was afraid that I too, would be taken from him. He touched me with a desperation that I had never experienced. He cradled me like a porcelain doll that would break with the slightest movement. His heart beat furiously, and when my cheeks touched his, I could feel their wetness.

He grew accustomed to my silence. Indeed, Simon spoke to me as if nothing had changed, interpreting the slightest of my gestures as the voice of his wife. He watched the flickering of my eyelids, and listened for the tremors of my spirit. If I stirred in my sleep, he would cradle me. If I stopped weaving, he would scrutinize the rows of flax swaying in our garden, hastening the day of harvest. Or he might tempt the shepherd with the choicest specimens of fish for wool. I carded the wool, dried the flax, and wove the pain away.

Nights I wandered the frothing shores of Lake Gennesaret. The water was a void. Waves licked at my feet and I saw in them the salivating, tantalizing hunger of a mother. I kicked the waves violently, only to receive a cold splashing. I continued kicking, spraying myself with beads of seawater. Salt became trapped in my eyes, rendering them too sore for tears. There was a burning in my eyes, like boils beneath my eyelids, and I wished I was blind, blind to the sea that thrust my bitter loss into my face, that cynical sea laughing over my failure to bear a child.

The moon was cold and radiant; the sea shimmered in the constant surge forward, each wave disappearing as the next enveloped the shore. Phantoms danced in the sea's silvery convulsions. Then it seemed the entire lake was whirling. Tiny fingers reached out to me under the turmoil, and tiny feet were thrashing. *My son! My son!*

Then he was gone, and I was tired. The water drew my strength and I gave myself to the waves, allowing the current to carry me wherever it might. The lake engulfed me, smooth as a caress, and I was disappearing. I was sinking and floating at the same time, waiting for Death to claim me and reunite me with Bar-Simon. The water licked at my face, covering my nose, and soon my breath would be quenched. *Peace, at last.*

Then lights blinked, as the neighbors' oil lamps were nocturnally aroused and taken off their nails. Soon my husband came running, and my mother after him, hair disarrayed and all. Villagers snickered at the half-mad wife of Simon the fisherman, raving about the temperamental lake. I let them talk. My son was dead. I had become dead, and the dead cared nothing for rumors.

—————

My naked feet felt the sting of the sand, each grain heated by the throbbing sun at midday. The sun beat down on my uncovered face, and my perspiration ran in rivers along my back. Lake Gennesaret seemed like a mirage in the distance, a blinking cobalt eye. I felt suddenly exposed before the sea and the sun and the heavenly eyes of God. Raw, broken, and inadequate. Pain awakened me to his burning wrath.

Then I heard a rustling nearby, along the empty dock. All the fishermen were supposed to be fishing in the deep waters at the height of noon, and rarely did they return unless the nets failed or they rendered a miraculous catch. I discerned the tall, slight figure of John at the shoreline. He intently surveyed the sand, appearing to retrieve stray hooks. I wondered how the men had managed to be so careless as to leave rusting hooks strewn along the shore, poisoning the blood of those unfortunate enough to stumble upon those nasty metallic fangs.

John was so captivated by his task that he did not see me as the waves lapped onto the beach and his feet became wet. His cheeks grew crimson in his concentration, and his pallid complexion seemed almost rosy. He bent over several more times, collected more, closed his sack, and then hurried toward the dock. Except, he walked past the dock toward the village, and I followed him on the path, intrigued despite myself.

He made a few strides towards the village along the main thoroughfare that everyone used to come to Capernaum, but then he veered right onto a small trail marked by an olive tree. The grasses grew thicker, and more olive trees appeared in a grove, with few shafts of sunlight filtering through the lofty branches. The wind rustled the leaves, and John began to whistle, his own fluty breath a pitch lower than the warblers, and it seemed they were singing the same song.

A small ridge became visible as John rounded the trail, and he walked with great familiarity into the mouth of the rock—and disappeared. It must have been a cave, and gingerly I followed him into the opening. It was a small alcove inside, only a few cubits in each dimension, so that the space was no larger than the smallest room in Simon's house. Upon the ledges of rock were seashells of all shapes and sizes, shimmering as if they had been polished with oil.

John spun around, startled, and dropped his bag. Out scattered not hooks, but a lone chiton shell and a few clam shells, still moist. I shook my head sheepishly and gazed at his myriad collection with wonder.

He let out a breath and smiled a bit apologetically. "I… I didn't know anyone was watching. The catch was slow today, so I… well, I have been collecting seashells for years. There is much beauty, even in the smallest of worlds." He picked up a snail shell, speckled and brown as molasses. "There are worlds within worlds. The earth, the sea, the shells, they all have a message for us, if we would listen."

My skepticism must have registered on my face. John looked at me, his eyes the shade of an opalescent dawn, violent undertones of a pure, unblemished blue. Still a youth, flaxen fuzz surrounded his firm chin and the thin line of his mouth, the beginnings of a beard.

He took a step back and he picked up a nondescript seashell. "I know you have suffered. I have felt your pain." His eyes fell to my belly, which was flat and shriveled under layers of tunics and cloaks. "It has not been for nothing."

John reached out and gave me the seashell. "Open it."

I twisted it with all my might and it stubbornly refused to open.

"Hold it at the thickest part of shell. There." He pointed. "Now twist it quickly."

I followed his instructions and broke it open. Inside, I

found a luminescent pearl, pale and round and perfect.

I looked up. John was beaming.

"Pearls are congealed oyster spit. Only through great pressure and pain does the saliva become a pearl. You must learn from the oyster."

Oyster in hand, I ran back to the house. Breathless, I searched for my husband. We embraced without words, and later he lifted me tenderly onto the pallet, enveloping me in his warmth, the familiarity of his perspiration, bristles of his beard. We kissed and touched with abandon, the stars and the heavens satiating our own drought, finding ourselves and each other again.

CHAPTER VI

Zebedee the fisherman fell ill. It was not a surprise, since the elderly father of James and John had a delicate constitution, prone to outbreaks of fever and boils. For this reason, Zebedee had entrusted his sons to my father Ephraim, as apprentices to learn the trade of fishing. James assumed leadership of daily operations in his father's stead, while John had taken to expanding the business among new customers near and far. During his forays into Jerusalem, John had managed to acquire the goodwill of the high priest of Jerusalem for the quality of his catch. Soon, more hands were required for the salting of fish and carts of sardines, musht, sprat, mackerel, and twenty other varieties of fish delivered to the Great Temple thrice a year.

With Zebedee's decline, the responsibilities of James and John were doubled, as they needed to manage their father's business in addition to their expanding commerce. With the support of my husband and Andrew, the partners decided to consolidate Zebedee's fishing enterprise with their own. Simon threw himself into work with an abandon. He was obsessed with every detail of the fishing expansion. The death of my father had ended the staggering bride-price disbursements and with newfound resources from Zebedee, my husband was eager to invest. He spent hours hiring and training new fisherman, leading excursions in the deep waters and accounting for their wages. Often he was too exhausted to talk and collapsed into a deep slumber beside me. He seemed desperate to be occupied and did not allow himself a spare moment for leisure. Andrew found himself chastised for suggesting that my husband rest. Simon became a slave to his ambition, the dream of prosperity.

The fishing partnership expanded beyond his expectations. John decided to target the noble houses and mercantile classes as potential customers, while James began training new apprentices. Andrew enlisted the help of another bookkeeper to track the growing accounts, and Simon planned an expansion of the enterprise toward the processing of fish. I was curious, and so my husband took me to visit fish-processing centers to jointly learn the trade.

We traveled to Magdala, a few leagues south of Capernaum, where the majority of processing installations were located. So I learned how fish could be cured, pickled, dried, and preserved for transportation, or mixed with wine during fermentation. I saw the spice and life wrung out of fish, becoming a black liquid saltier than the Dead Sea. Garum was made by placing entrails of small whole fish, like smelts, tiny mullets, or anchovies into a vat, and salting all of it. Then it was dried in the sun, aged by heat. After this, a long, thickly woven basket was placed into the vat; garum was strained through the basket and then extracted. The remaining sediment was allec, and gathered for future use.

Because Simon was intent on identifying the optimal methods of processing fish, we visited multiple processing houses. The Bithynians used a similar method, requiring fewer ingredients to produce garum. They put sprats, lizard fish, allec, or a mixture of all these into a trough usually used for kneading dough. Two sextarii of salt were added to each modius of fish, and stirred well so that it was thoroughly mixed. The mixture was then transferred to clay vats and placed uncovered in the sun for two or three months, stirred occasionally with sticks. Afterward, the concoction was bottled, sealed, and stored. The addition of two sextarii of old wine per sextarius of fish was optional, only if a richer flavor was desired.

I preferred the Bithynian way. I wanted to maintain the integrity of the body without separation, placating that which was once alive. Through the heavy labor of stirring, perspiration would drip into the troughs; the sweat of man and juice of fish combined into one creation that would outlast both its predecessors.

My husband also preferred the Bithynian method of processing fish, but for different reasons. It was by far the most economical, requiring much less salt than the Judean method, and was possible to make even with lower-grade fish. Additionally, the investment in equipment would be lower, as he would not need to purchase the baskets used in the Judean method. His excitement showing in his eyes, Simon began calculating the investment needed in the purchase of salt, wine, amphorae, and olive oil, which had to be supplied by farmers and merchants in Jerusalem. Yet Simon was not satisfied with vicarious reports from traders regarding variety and price. He hated middlemen. He needed to examine the goods and bargain with merchants himself, evaluating their faces for any semblances of deceit. It seemed a journey to Jerusalem was inevitable.

With trepidation, Simon prepared for an excursion to assess oils and other necessary ingredients for fish processing. My husband usually avoided the sojourn to the metropolis due to the multitude of pilgrimages. With every religious festival, myriad caravans traveled to the city of glittering limestone and the Feast of Unleavened Bread was approaching. I would accompany my husband, crossing out of Galilee into the unwelcoming land of Judea. Despite sharing one God, Judeans regarded their northern brethren as bumpkins, incapable of understanding the finer things in life. They were city folk, educated in Aramaic and Greek, condescending to us villagers. Even our accent was repugnant to them.

———

None of the others entertained the journey to Jerusalem with excitement. Andrew assented after much deliberation, a growing curiosity to see a new prophet called John the Baptist along the banks of the river Jordan. The younger son of Zebedee cited his responsibility to his ailing father, and the need to keep watch over the ever-growing fishing enterprise. John was none too ecstatic about the crowds of pilgrims pushing and milling about, and antagonistic Judeans who would look at him as a fly in their stew. James made the most excuses for staying behind, his starry eyes entranced by a far more tangible wonder. Cana was his favored destination, a lively town known for flowing wells, pretty pastures, and even prettier girls. One pretty girl in particular had caught his eye. The colossus grinned and turned red as a beet when asked about the object of his affection. "She's a shepherdess. She is in the Cana village marketplace once a week, selling young goats and lambs. I try to be in the marketplace when she is there."

Simon rolled his eyes, as all the partners did when they contemplated the giant's latest infatuation. James's attention was bestowed and waned easily, like the passing fancies of an adolescent boy, although he was far beyond boyhood. His appetite for drink was equally voracious, even as he lifted his jug and gulped while we talked. Swallowing, James clicked his tongue and inquired about the evening's dinner.

His mother, old Salome was glad to indulge her elder son's cravings, even more ecstatic that he chose to forego the festivities of Jerusalem for the sleepiness of

102

Capernaum. She confided that she had trouble keeping him at home and perhaps only a wife would do to keep him close, but no suitable wife could be found. She never mentioned John and his habitual roaming of the woods, but for James, she scoured the neighboring villages of Bethsaida and Magdala for a beautiful and obedient girl, beautiful enough to retain her son's interest and obedient enough to maintain her rigorous household. She even enlisted my help, but I knew no one for him.

My husband worried about leaving the fishing enterprise, despite the hefty presence of James and the serenity of John to quell their hired laborers of any unfortunate thoughts of cheating the bosses. It was Andrew who did the meticulous bookkeeping, who watched the flow of supplies, and who counted the intake of fish after every excursion. It was Simon who ultimately held the laborers accountable for their catch. Simon had assessed each man's strength and talent, assessed how much labor each was worth. It seemed he feared a mutiny. I reassured him that James was adequate to contend with any challenge, along with the army of apprentices he trained. James had cultivated loyalty; the apprentices were his eyes and ears, which the hired men feared more than the wrath of the giant himself. They even hid his indiscretions voluntarily, despite the pleas of desperate girls believing themselves in love with the colossus. Secretly, they must have envied this careless fellow, so capable with his hands that nets obeyed his whim and fish came his way.

———

The day of departure, while watering the two camels that Simon had hired at extravagant prices for the journey, I thought of tasks left to be completed before daybreak when the journey would officially begin. A host of pilgrims left Galilee at this time every year, to pay tribute to Jerusalem, the holy city of God's people. My husband was going to pursue yet another fancy—the vision of processing fish—and left practical matters to me. I packed supplies of food, counting nuts and grains, stashing ample quantities of salted fish. Water bags were necessary for crossing the desert, and mats for sleeping in the caravansaries. There were cooking utensils to bring—a small kettle and cauldron for boiling water—and extra clothing, because the rainy season was not yet over and we might need to spend some nights out in the open.

Sunrise bathed the horizon in deepening hues of rose. I mounted one camel; the other was laden with provisions. Most of the men in our company walked. Simon, however, was concerned I would not be able to withstand rigors of the journey, and walked alongside me. My husband was engaged in a conversation with Andrew, who kept his eyes on the ground, skirting around sharp-edged stones that littered the path.

As we reached the outskirts of Capernaum, it became clear that we would not be on our own. Several large families were making a pilgrimage to Jerusalem, three generations of a single clan, including elders, boisterous young men, and small children. My heart fluttered as the children ran to and fro, loitering at some flower or butterfly and then running ahead, impatient to reach the destination.

The lush greenery, orange and pomegranate trees, and rolling hills faded as the Plain of Gennesaret grew farther in the distance, and even the blinking of threshing farmers ceased. Great rocks came into view, sloping gradually into the eastern mountains of Samaria. The winds began to change, arid desert air suffocating us as we traversed the well-traveled path between great mountains and a great river, specks of dust in the ever-fluctuating boundaries of Israel.

The trees also changed, perhaps out of loyalty to the sienna-colored earth in which they were rooted. Clumps of date palms and fig trees appeared sporadically along the periphery of the desert. We felt the scorching of the land as we walked, and anticipated the raging animosity of the Samaritans. They hated us, all Galileans. Descendants of the ancient Assyrians, the Samaritans settled in these parts after the expulsion of the ten tribes, under the king of Nineveh. They barely acknowledged the Five Books of Moses as Sacred Law. To them, the Holy Scriptures suggested that God's chosen temple was on the summit of Mount Gerizim, not Jerusalem. To them, all others were heretics.

We moved across Samaria with anxiety, the men tensing their bodies for any act of hostility or ambush on the part of natives. The men divided themselves into two contingents, one in the front and one in the back, to protect women and children from taunts or insults, or worse. Robbers were known to frequent these paths, and their treachery knew no bounds. Travelers told of dying Galileans, and Samaritans refusing to give them a drink of water, even at their last breaths. The pace was brisk, like refugees fleeing war, and many of our company cut their feet, bleeding and developing sores. Even so, we could not avoid spending three nights in enemy territory.

At night, while traversing Samaria, the men set up patrols to guard the expedition. There was no conversation, no laughter, and no stories around the hearth. Even the fire was kept at a minimum and stamped out after the cooking concluded. Nights were cold, but no one complained. Infants were hushed, and the mutterings of the elders were stifled. For three nights, no one slept save the children, and we lay waiting in silence. For unknown reasons, the inhabitants of Samaria did not attack. We marveled at our luck as we approached Judea; there was no aggression, and no gang of robbers descending from the mountains to pelt us with rocks.

Dusk settled on our final night in the wilderness. Everyone was in a foul mood, the tension of Samaria building in our bones, palpable in our voices. I prepared supper with the other women, the mothers querulous among themselves. Even the children grew cantankerous, picking fights, and neighbors tired of prying them from each other. Finishing my part, I retreated to a quiet corner. My heart felt disturbed.

One night, from where I sat, I could see my husband's profile against the light of the fire. Half of his face was in shadow; the glowering reflection of flames traced his features, making him appear angry. His mouth puckered sullenly over a wild conflagration of a beard, and his shoulders slumped. With surprise, I realized that my husband was not an attractive man. It was his impish grin beneath that prickly beard that had captivated me. Now he just looked morose. Simon watched the fire with contemplative eyes, as if by gazing long enough he could ascertain truth.

Andrew sat beside him. Simon spoke toward the fire, gesturing with his arms, and his brother nodded. The younger son of Jonah then replied with muted words, and my husband frowned. Simon wrung his fingers and took a deep breath, as if making a concession. I knew better than to approach them. Their legs were juxtaposed against each other, while the brothers were making a deal.

The embers were dying. My husband looked up and searched for me, expecting food. I brought a bowl of thin barley soup to his lap, and another to Andrew. Simon began eating immediately, but his brother pushed away his bowl and sighed. Then my husband frowned at his empty wineskin, and he rose to walk toward a large family of hefty boys. The sky was darkening, plumes of violet spreading over the heavens like a blanket. In the distance, stars began to twinkle.

I lingered near Andrew, and when Simon was out of earshot, I said, "So you will be leaving us tomorrow morning."

Andrew nodded. "Yes."

"When will you be returning?"

"In five days. Simon and I will meet along the banks of the river Jordan, three leagues east of Jerusalem."

I decided to inquire further, having heard of the man Andrew wanted to meet: "The Baptizer?"

"Yes."

"They say he is a heretic, a fugitive."

Andrew looked beyond me, his gaze fixated on Simon. For the first time, Andrew was not following his elder brother. He nodded slowly.

I eyed him. "Why do you want to meet him?"

He poked at the charred remains of the fire, blackened wood crumbling into cinders. "Simon asked me the same question, fearing the needless danger. I cannot say exactly. I have felt…disquiet. My life has somehow lost meaning. Somehow I have faded and everything seems…indefinite. Somehow I have outgrown all the old habits. This monotony of waking, fishing, eating, sleeping…this endless cycle repeating. Is this everything life will be? I have nothing to look forward to. I am tired. Something feels amiss."

Andrew tossed a pebble into the hearth, and the ashes stirred. I had never seen Andrew so...agitated... discontent.

When he looked at me again, his eyes reflected hope. "Somehow, I believe if I meet the Baptizer, things will be different. I don't know much about him, actually. I am just not sure what I believe anymore."

———

Early the next morning, after Andrew had gone on his way, Simon and I rode the camels on the remaining leg of the journey. We had exhausted our provisions and the camels were otherwise significantly relieved of their load. The road was rocky, jostling me in the saddle while my husband rode alongside me protectively. The burning plain of Judea stretched southward, the sun beating down our necks. I sniffed the air, inhaling the sweetness of Jerusalem.

Years ago, as a young girl, I had been on a journey like this, riding my father's carriage with Leta. I remembered Jerusalem, the golden city, rising with the sun. Limestone glittered like ivory, heavenly walls built from heavenly stone, and I loved each one. In my joy, I kissed Leta on the lips, and I would have kissed the ground if I had been close enough. When Leta wiped my saliva from her mouth, I laughed with abandon and told her to pretend that I was a man. If I were a man, I could study in the Great Temple in Jerusalem. If I were a man, I could pass through barricades of the Court of Women, into the Court of the Jews. If I were a man and the high priest, I could walk upon sacred ground and enter into the Holy of Holies, where God lived. If I were a man, I could meet God.

My reverie was broken by the chattering and pointing of children. The Holy City came into sight like an apparition, nestled on the crest of a hill beyond the valley. "Jerusalem, Jerusalem," the travelers chanted, "the most exquisite city on earth." A hush followed, the respectful silence that the city of God demanded. The Temple towered like a crown jewel, a place between heaven and earth that bore the footprints of Yahweh, and the everlasting breath of the Lord that blows his creatures every which way. Trembling with emotion, the pilgrims lifted their eyes to where the Temple touched the sky, and raised their arms as if touching divinity, each lost in his own ecstasy. The pious among our company prayed fervently, hoping that God could hear them at last in this sacred space.

Even Simon mouthed a prayer. He saw me watching him, then blinked and rubbed his eyes as if to remove wayward grains of sand. I found my lips were too stiff to pray. Perhaps I did not believe that God was listening. Then the road plunged downward into the valley, and we had to climb the next slope to reach the city gates. All the while, the Temple rose higher and higher, adjacent to the sinister Antonia fortress, guarded by Roman soldiers armed to the teeth with spears and swords. At the same time, the pilgrims with us began singing psalms—the Songs of Ascent—as they climbed upward.

At the city's edge, our traveling company parted ways once inside the Fish Gate—aptly named for our reason for journeying. Some pilgrims headed straight toward the Temple for prayers and sacrifices, while others wandered through the labyrinthine lanes, searching for an inn to rest their feet. I was glad to be on the camel's back. The city seethed with bazaars, animals, and people of all kinds, and a plethora of languages reverberated in the air. The odor pervading the crowds was the universally recognized musk of sweat. Drunkards roamed the streets, patrolled sporadically by Romans with cavalier helmets and disdainful faces. Beggars huddled in corners, the sick and lame spreading their infirmities out for all to see. Nobles came and went in carriages, curtains flapping airily like butterflies. In every direction, waves of human extremities assailed me like an army, and I felt suffocated by the torrent of man's greed: taking, selling, grabbing, and begging.

I felt nauseated by all of it. My husband inquired about the way to the stall of a Phoenician salt merchant, with whom he had an appointment. Slaves were bartered as we passed. Prostitutes swaggered their uncovered heads at Simon and jingled their bangles; country folk usually meant easy business, after all. It would have seemed surreal if not for the sickening of my stomach and the chill that penetrated my bones. That morning's meal churned in my belly and I clasped both hands over my mouth to keep from retching. Simon kept saying that the salt merchant was just around the next corner. Our movements were so painstakingly slow, I felt as if I would explode.

Finally, I jumped down from the camel and relieved myself of the tumultuous juices that agonized my stomach. White mush spilled over the cobbled pathway, dribbling from my mantle, and passersby leaped aside to avoid the onslaught. I wiped my mouth and clothes with my kerchief, surveying the damage. A fruit vendor held his nose and gave me a menacing glance, as if his stock of elderberries were inseparable from my vomit. Then I heard a familiar laugh. A pair of fine leather sandals appeared beneath my nose. I lifted my head—and groaned within.

Hasar.

He was accompanied by two slaves, one leading a horse such exquisite conformation that it must have once belonged to nobility. Hasar himself aspired to nobility. His lavish banquets were the toast of Jerusalem, known for exotic Egyptian entertainments involving pagan rituals and slave girls. I heard of the fortune he amassed from processing fish sauces, and knew of how he engaged the tailors of Roman households for his togas. His robe, made of fine gossamer linen, was a bit too long for him and trailed behind him like a tail.

"How far you have fallen, daughter of Ephraim."

I rose to my full height. "Master Hasar. I am the wife of Simon bar Jonah now."

Holding the reins of his camel, Simon stepped between us and obstructed the fish merchant's gaze. "Shalom, Master Hasar. Our regrets, my wife and I have an appointment."

"Ah, yes…about that. I have just come from a meeting with Isaac the salt merchant. He has closed shop for the day. Urgent business in Phoenicia, you know. All appointments are cancelled."

My husband simply blinked, too shocked to speak.

So I voiced his bewilderment. "How did you know our destination?"

Hasar grinned. He spoke to my husband, but he looked at me: "Simon, my poor fellow, you have much to learn. Isaac is an old colleague. I have many friends in this industry. You will find all relevant merchants in Jerusalem are similarly detained." He bade us goodbye.

Hasar's words carried like a curse as we went on to our business. Wherever we knocked, the merchants were absent, ill, or about to conclude work for the day. No salt, olive oil, wine, or amphorae were available for sale. No one would even venture to quote prices to us. One oil merchant explicitly informed us that he could not conduct business with us at the risk of invoking the wrath of his primary customer in Galilee. Hasar was the largest consumer of condiments for fish sauce in the north. While the merchant spoke, slaves carried out jars brimming with oil, loading them onto a cart. Simon inquired of oil merchants outside Jerusalem, from whom he might purchase a small measure. The merchant shook his head, advising my husband to forego his intention of buying oil. No one would dare cross Hasar. Simon clenched his fists. I said nothing.

We dragged our camels across the bazaar, my beloved's footsteps heavy with dejection. We walked through cobblestoned streets lined with houses, and with fences offering glimpses of the gardens inside. The houses grew grander as the roads grew steeper along the dusty hillside, strewn with misshapen rocks. The wind was rough near the summit of the hill. The Temple stood unassailable, the glory of an insurmountable faith, rebuilt again after the destruction of the Assyrians. Its massive grounds were teaming with crowds offering sacrifices and sellers of animals flaunting their stock. It was only a few days before Passover. From a distance, I could see money-changing tables lining the Court of Gentiles, and clanking coins drowned out the sounds of prayer. Butchers brandished knives and hauled wailing lambs farther into the Temple's courtyards. I could smell the hot, pulsating blood that permeated the house of God. Prostitutes roamed a few paces from the Temple gates, awaiting weary men who needed to prove their manhood. At the entrance, Simon hesitated and looked at me. I shook my head. I felt too ill to enter another marketplace.

We mounted our camels and headed eastward toward the Salt Sea. The Kidron Valley opened to us in an abundance of olive groves, light filtering through the leaves in green transcendence. My stomach ceased roiling. Sweat gathered on Simon's brow, but his face appeared visibly relieved. We rode on as the sun began to descend, the Moab mountains looming higher and higher before us, a wall of rock. The mountains began to fade, passive ridges on the horizon that glowed pink, infused with the setting sun. The darkening began in the east, and we saw our destination clouded by purple shadows of the Moab mountains to the east. Dusk brought lethargy to the land, and the earth was falling asleep.

From a distance, there came a twinkling of lanterns. We heard the steady hum of laborers returning from work, collegial footsteps that melded into the passing of one day. The scent of threshed grain filled our nostrils. We were approaching Jericho, city of palm trees and plentiful springs, city of the Promised Land. After the bondage of Egypt, stories told of how Joshua and the Israelites waged a battle with the Canaanites here, shouting whereupon the walls crumbled. The fertility of the region was legendary. Jericho was burnt to the ground, with a curse put upon it, but resurrected thousands of years later by Herod the Great, who built aqueducts and a hippodrome theater. Date plantations stretched across the plain, and beyond were cottages lit by flickering oil lamps. I looked toward the city, but Simon gestured toward a remote clump of sycamore trees.

"We can gather dates from the trees and settle here for the night. It should take another day's journey to the river Jordan."

"I would rather find an inn in the city. We have been nomads for days."

"It is easier to depart from here than from the center of the city. Besides, our resources are low."

"The hospitality of Jericho is well known. I'm sure a kind artisan would offer us lodging for the night."

"I will not accept charity, woman. Here we will stay."

I raised an eyebrow. "And pilfer dates?"

Simon grunted in response, coloring to the tips of his ears. I unpacked the necessities with a heavy hand, and we settled into our makeshift tents and mats. As my eyes closed, I heard my husband's watchful breathing.

———

Light was blinding when we awoke; the sun was a steaming disc in the sky. Simon picked dates for me to eat, plump and bursting with juice. Jericho was once a love gift from Mark Antony to Cleopatra, a playground for immortals. Springs spouted forth from the ground; ostentatious roses bloomed, tangled in the grasses that outnumbered them. Paradise must look like this.

Jericho was awakening; shepherds were leading flocks out to pasture and laborers went out to the plantations to begin gathering the fruit. The sky was reflected in copious streams that collected water from the springs, blue and deep. I brought water to Simon, who washed his face and drank heartily. As I came back to drink, I dropped my cup with a splash and it drifted downstream. I followed it down the sloping hill and came upon a man gulping from the stream. He drank as if he could never quench his thirst, and water leaked from the trough of his hands.

"Please, sir, my cup!" I said, pointing.

With the advantage of height and long willowy arms, he retrieved it with ease. Shading his eyes with the one hand, he squinted against the blaring sun. Then he smiled and gave me the cup.

"Woman, let me drink from your cup."

Galilean. A wave of neighborly affection swept over me. I filled the cup with water and gave it to the man. He drank, and then he laughed. His was a slow-blossoming smile. His hair was long, but kempt, and his few whiskers were bleached by the sun. His features were nondescript except for the eyes. They were the color of earth, of amber illuminated. Deep wells of understanding.

I shifted my gaze to his feet. They were broad and well-proportioned, blistered from constant rupture with the thongs of his sandals. His skin was peeling, whorls of sunburned brown and naked red alternating on his wide, tired feet. His toes were gray from gravel and dust; his toenails were the pale pink of a seashell. His feet belonged to a nomad, one who traveled far and wide. I began to wonder about the marvelous things he had seen, the

117

stories he could tell.

I had never seen so much sweetness in a man.

Then I heard my husband calling me. In a few seconds, Simon had climbed over the hill and eyed me talking to a stranger. Simon approached, his chin jutting out.

"We need to cross the desert before noon," he said to me.

The stranger gazed at Simon, standing shorter by a head. "Is your destination the Jordan?"

Simon nodded, surprised.

The man surveyed the sky and then uncovered some grapes from his pack. He offered them to us.

"It will be a taxing journey; I hope these will be a source of comfort."

My husband glanced at the large, luscious grapes and seemed to change his mind. "Friend, are you also headed to the Dead Sea?"

The stranger grinned. "I am seeking a distant relative. I hear he has become a baptizer, a prophet, but I have never met him."

"My brother also seeks the prophet," Simon grumbled. "His curiosity has gotten the better of him, and I am tasked with bringing him home. Since we are journeying to the same place, come, let us travel together. We are all brothers far from home. My name is Simon bar Jonah and I am from Capernaum. I can tell you are also from Galilee. What is your name?"

"I am Jesus, from the village of Nazareth."

CHAPTER VII

So Jesus accompanied us to the river Jordan. He often sat in deep contemplation and prayer, yet his laughter rang so merrily that it was contagious. I also discerned an inquisitiveness in him, and he reasoned with the logic of one trained in the Law. He asked many questions and seemed particularly interested in what we thought. He and Simon conversed at length about politics, and he often glanced at me for my opinions, though I had few to give. I was content with listening. At the day's end, I listened to Jesus's voice and my husband's stammering speech above the crackling fire. Our new friend had many tales to tell.

Jesus had been a continental wanderer after the death of his father, a carpenter who was crushed by falling beams in the construction of Sepphoris. Jesus had not returned to Nazareth for several years. He traveled about the Empire, from Egypt to Ephesus to Rome. He spoke of a mountain spewing fire outside of the port city of Pompeii, and how Ethiopians pierced their noses with ivory and gold. He even ventured to the northern regions of Gaul, where insurgents ambushed Roman legionaries and stuck their severed heads on pikes.

Simon perked up at the mention of insurrection, but I

was fascinated by the journey, the searching. Our friend had the courage to turn away from life's demands to follow a yearning.

"What were you looking for?" I spoke before I stopped myself.

Simon glared at me, but Jesus did not seem surprised.

"I want to understand why—why men sin and why they die."

"Scripture says that men die because of sin," Simon said. "We all suffer because of Adam, and his fall into temptation. Women, of course, are the root of it all."

I said nothing, deciding to let Simon and Jesus discuss it while I listened.

"Yes." Jesus sighed. "So it is written."

"You do not seem content with what is written," I said.

"There is so much suffering in the world," Jesus said. "What could be done?"

"Do not sin," Simon replied flippantly.

Jesus gave my husband a grave look and he fell silent.

"All people sin," Jesus said. "Even if they repent, could they ever be free of sin? There must be more than judgment. There must be a merciful way."

"What's the difference?" Simon said. "God punishes anyway."

Jesus stopped at the bitterness in Simon's voice. "My friend, why do you think so?"

"You have seen the suffering yourself. Is it not

121

obvious?"

"Why blame God for human suffering?"

"Why is God silent while his people suffer? Look at the wars, disease, and death. What about the poor and blind, infants who die in their mothers' wombs, and soldiers fighting a war they did not cause? Many of these things are beyond our control, where those who suffer are innocent." My husband bit his lip. His eyes, the shade of ash, smoldered at the thought of injustice.

"Innocent of what?" Jesus asked quietly.

"Innocent of wrongdoing."

"Only God can determine that."

Simon cringed. "I just want to know why God allows people to suffer."

Jesus stared at him, then asked, "Why do you think it is God?"

"If not God, then who?"

Now Jesus looked at Simon sadly. "God gave men free will. Adam broke away from God's order and introduced disobedience onto this earth. That disorder, that lawlessness beyond God's reign, is what causes suffering. The choices we make cause suffering. Our expectations cause suffering. The world's imperfections cause suffering. It is inevitable. To live is to suffer."

Simon shook his head. "Why do I have to share responsibility? I am innocent of that sin."

"We all share responsibility in that sin. Being human, we are inextricably linked to that sin. It is in our blood.

The question is not why we suffer, but…"

"… what we learn from our suffering?" I spoke despite myself.

Jesus nodded. "The world is in need of healing. Our own pain allows us to touch others in a miraculous way. Because you were broken, you can mend the hearts of others. Because you were sick, you can rejuvenate the sick. Because you were poor, you can console those in poverty. Because you were blind, you can bring vision to the sightless. Because you were hopeless, you are able to instill hope."

The carpenter's son put his hand on Simon's shoulder. "Because I lost a father, I can share in your loss."

My husband trembled. "I lost my firstborn son. I could not save him."

I held my breath. My husband never mentioned Bar-Simon.

"You have a purpose, Simon, son of Jonah," Jesus said, just above a whisper.

Simon buried his head in his hands and cried. My heart beat wildly and I felt palpitations in my jaw. I was in the presence of a prophet.

———

It was nearly dusk when we reached the Dead Sea, our tongues too parched for speech. Jesus had lapsed into silence, meditating on the skies. My husband was sulking over having lost his attention, and even the pressure of my

123

arms wrapped around his waist did not mollify him. The camels treaded with a lethargy, brought on by the intense heat. The waves rolled sluggishly to the shore, heavy with salt. In the shadows, it seemed we were looking into a pool of molasses. On the eastern shore stood a solitary tree, obscured by an irregularly shaped crag. We approached it, and the stone formation divided into two flanks outstretched like wings. The camels halted.

"This is where Andrew said to meet," Simon murmured, looking about, "but we came early."

Jesus climbed down from the camel and perused the rocky shores, twisted tree, and the sea in which all fish perished. The sand was dotted with clumps of wild grass. He sniffed the air and sneezed, perhaps at the stink of salt. In the distance, crickets stirred.

"This is the camp of the Baptizer?" Jesus asked.

"This is the meeting point," Simon said. "I think the camp is farther, but I am not sure how far."

"It must be along the river, where he baptizes," Jesus said. "Let's walk farther."

We dismounted and walked past the rock, past the Dead Sea. The stars began to appear, and Jesus pointed northward. I looked at him with wonder. He smiled and mentioned an Egyptian sailor who taught him the constellations and the North Star.

We followed Jesus into a wall of reeds, plunging our feet into the marshy lands of the riverbank. It was slippery and my ankle tickled, so I shook it, but the teasing sensation did not abate. I glanced down and let out a shriek. A silver asp had coiled around my ankle, moving slowly along my calf. It hissed, lifting its head from my body so that it seemed to be standing erect.

Simon paled, paralyzed by fear. "Do not move."

Jesus plucked a thick reed and slowly placed it along my leg. He gazed at the reptile and it looked back at him with beady eyes, hissing. He gave a low, long whistle and shook the reed slightly. The asp hissed again and reluctantly crawled onto the reed, its metallic body undulating. Jesus set it down in the slimy water and it scurried away, flaunting an elongated tail.

I took a deep breath. My body was still trembling. Then I heard indignant cries coming our way:

"The nerve! We came to his baptism and he called us hypocrites!"

"Look at how bony he is; he eats nothing but honey."

"He talks above us! No one is above the holy priests of God! We are not the ones needing repentance."

"It shows we cannot believe what commoners think!"

"Brood of vipers, indeed!"

A congregation of men broke through the reeds, flicking the plants away from their fine robes—and I knew from their dress that these were Pharisees and Sadducees. The Pharisees were an austere group, most knowledgeable about the Torah, and strict observers of Mosaic Law. The Sadducees were keepers of the Great Temple, a religious group comprised of the aristocratic class and other high

125

ranking officials from Judean society, with a certain fondness for Hellenistic principles. Flustered in their choler, they were red-faced and their cloaks were drenched in perspiration. Gold chains jingled around their necks, and they held their togas to their waists to avoid the mud. At the sight of us, they stopped and smoothed their garments. Then they straightened and lifted their heads, slinking past like proud young lions.

We kept walking. In the distance, we saw a man in a robe, his back facing us. There was something familiar in the way he held his shoulders, and his halting footsteps. Simon began to run ahead.

"Brother!" he called out.

Andrew turned around, his face sunburned. "Simon! You are early. I did not expect you for a few days."

My husband nodded his greeting, "I brought a friend—Jesus of Nazareth."

———

The tents were situated in a camp deep in the wilderness. Here, the yellow dust churned with expectation and prophecies. Here, eagles circled the sky, crying exultation for the One who was to come. Here, date trees hovered, their fruits sustaining pilgrims seeking baptism. Here, leaves and balsam ameliorated the weary. Here, the night was long, stretching into a silence that was grave as the desert air was cold. Here, we waited, anticipating the morrow.

126

Simon tossed and turned throughout the night. The sound of Jesus's breathing was ragged, and I wondered if he was sleeping. As the darkness began to subside, my husband's snoring began. Then I heard shuffling footsteps and saw Jesus tiptoeing toward the tent's opening. He tripped over Simon's gangly legs, but my husband did not stir. When Jesus disappeared outside, I followed.

The sky was the flat gray of clay. In the west, rays of moonshine illuminated Jesus as he wove throughout the trees. He moved with impressive speed; I panted to keep an observable distance behind him. Despite a well-traveled road toward the river, Jesus climbed over boulders and skirted brambles in the wilderness. I followed and scraped my knees.

The sun rose into an austere sky. I pushed through reeds and muddy waters, and finally the river Jordan came into view. Jesus walked to the shallow edge of the river and dipped his feet into the waters. He took off a sandal and knelt down, washing his feet. Due to the heat, a haze rose above the river, and the carpenter's son looked fuzzy to the eye. A group of disciples and a tall, gaunt man approached from the opposite direction. Andrew was among them. They were preparing for prayer, as the leader instructed them in a rumbling voice—The Baptizer, I knew. They stopped, noticing the stranger in their midst, who was now washing his face in the river. Visibly agitated, the most eager of the disciples rushed forth to ask the stranger to leave in reverence of the Baptizer's benediction. They stopped as their leader held up a bony hand.

This man, clothed in the soft raiment of a camel, came close to Jesus and asked him questions. Jesus answered with calm. I was too far to hear; indeed, the disciples leaned their bodies and strained their ears to catch the words. The Baptizer paled and bowed to Jesus, who shook his head. Jesus then gestured to the water, and the Judean prophet seemed bewildered. He protested, and Jesus spoke a few more words before he nodded. Both men walked farther down the river Jordan. I followed behind the reeds; Andrew and the other disciples followed on the opposite bank.

They stopped when they reached a small alcove where the river formed a pool. Ripples softened the cerulean surface, the two men multiplied by their reflections. Jesus stood in front of the water, and closed his eyes when the Baptizerblessed him. Then Jesus walked forward into the water, rapt in meditation as he took each step. Sapphire waters swirled around him as he walked into greater depths until his entire body was immersed by the river. He disappeared, and I began to fear that he had drowned, but he slowly walked back onto the shore. Rivulets of water ran down his body, gleaming silver upon his hair and the battered tunic he wore. The Baptizer knelt before him and held his sandals.

The sky seemed to rumble, but there were no clouds. A bird flew across the river between the two men and perched on a tree overlooking the Jordan. It was a dove unfurling its wings, feathers white and blinding. For a moment, it seemed to overpower the sun. Then it flew off.

Then the Baptizer called his disciples, who gathered in a circle around him. They began grinning from ear to ear, growing very excited. Jesus seemed taken aback by the attention and retreated along the river. His eyes were fixated toward heaven. I followed and strained to decipher his murmuring, but no words were clear to me.

I walked back to the baptism on the river. By now, throngs of crowds had pushed their way to the alcove. They came crying and shouting and lamenting, some for their families and most for themselves. The Baptizer ministered to the needy, and his disciples prepared them for the rite of baptism. I stood on the side, but as their numbers increased, the crowd swept me into its ranks. I found myself standing face-to-face with the Baptizer, John bar Zechariah, John the Baptist.

He was a tall man. His flesh wasted away by severe fasting, he had been sunburned with such frequency that his skin was rougher than bark. Raised by the Essenes, the order of priests known for their Spartan ways, John had abstained from meat and drink since childhood. Even his hair had never been cut. He seemed a skeleton, yet his voice was the stuff of thunder. He inspired fear and awe and distaste all at once. He was a man of spirit, or what spirit would look like bereft of all the pleasures of living.

"Repent!" he said. "Repent your sins now, for the day

of judgment is coming!"

He smelled of honey and it was more profuse than perfume. A trio of bees hovered about him, buzzing furiously, but he did not notice. They moved whenever he moved, as if bound to the thick scent of honey that emanated from his flesh. I feared they would sting, but they flew about as naturally as his shadow. He never once stopped to swat at them.

"Woman, what sins do you have to confess?" he asked me.

I could not think of a reply.

"The baptism cannot cleanse you if you do not repent your sins. What sins are in need of repentance?"

"Maybe the sin that caused my baby to die."

"Do you know what sin that is?"

"I do not. I do not understand why children have to suffer from the sins of their parents."

"You need to repent of your sins."

"I cannot repent from sins I have no knowledge of."

"Woman, you have not come in good faith. I cannot baptize you."

"But—"

"Repentance must be genuine. You do not even know your sins; how can you repent?"

"I do not know what made my baby die."

"Step aside, woman. There are many who are awaiting the baptism of God. Come back when you have learned to repent."

The angry bees buzzed and followed the Baptizer as he stepped away from me. His bellow carried downstream with such resonance that my cheeks reddened. The crowd gave me condescending stares. I wandered about the Jordan, avoiding the crowds. Hyraxes sunned themselves upon the rocks. Above me, skylarks called and falcons could be heard. Under the burning sun, I closed my eyes and listened to the rushing river. I thought of Jesus of Nazareth. Without knowing how my son had died, he had understood. He knew pain and loss and loneliness. He was the one I wanted to follow.

Then something jolted me and snapped me out of my reverie. I opened my eyes to see my husband shaking me. Andrew stood behind him. Both were more excited than I had ever seen them.

"Woman," Simon said, "where have you been? You have missed it!"

"Missed what?"

"We have found the One who will bring salvation," Andrew said.

My heart skipped a beat. "Who is he?"

"Jesus!" Simon said.

I tried to stand and promptly fell. I felt a tingling sensation in my legs, and my husband helped me up.

"How do you know?" I asked.

"This morning," Andrew said. "At the baptism. As Jesus of Nazareth conversed with the Baptizer, a voice came from heaven and a dove flew over his head. John prostrated himself before the Son of God. I brought Simon to his side right away." Andrew smiled at his brother.

Simon continued the tale. "Jesus said we were his friends. He was distressed that so many approached him—us along with disciples of the Baptizer. He seemed overwhelmed. He retreated into the desert and asked us not to follow him. There was something he needed to do alone. He said he needed to be tested. He said he will call us when it is time."

"Did he say anything else?" I whispered.

My husband nodded. "He told me that my name will be Simon Peter. I will become his rock. I will help him build his kingdom."

"Anything else?"

"He told me to rebuild my home."

That was all. I had hoped my name would be mentioned, a parting word from a friend. Perhaps Jesus forgot to mention me. Perhaps Simon forgot to tell me. Perhaps I was already forgotten.

CHAPTER VIII

A few days after our return to Capernaum, Simon announced that he would follow the word of Jesus and build me a house. He thought our hut was far too cramped for four people, and the proximity of the surf disturbed my slumber. My husband wanted something more spacious, and he began contracting with a stonecutter, builder, and carpenter immediately. I wrung my hands together, wondering where he would get the money.

"Your dowry."

I simply blinked at him in my bafflement.

"Your mother brought it when you were ill."

Behind him, light broke into the sky and the sun hung low on dawn's lavender horizon. Simon pulled a knapsack from the corner and unveiled a small casket. Upon opening it, trinkets gleamed in the wavering sunlight. I recognized them; they were the betrothal gifts of my own mother, bangles and rings my father had given to her as a bride price. I held up a gold bracelet, and looked at Simon.

He shrugged. "She said your brothers have already gotten their share. This was what she wanted to give you, and never could when your father was alive."

I scurried down the ladder and tripped over the bottom rungs, but my mother was nowhere in the house. Water was boiling in a cauldron outside, steam rising from the fire. The cock crowed. My mother was watering tall stalks of flax and blooming pomegranate trees, the very trees that had withered under my care. Tiny bulbs peeked through the leaves, green and ephemeral before they would deepen into ripe fruit.

"Amah."

I threw my arms around my mother, embracing her. She kissed both my cheeks.

The words tumbled from my mouth: "Simon told me about the dowry."

"Every time I thought about you, I added another piece to your dowry."

I suddenly felt ashamed. I only thought of her whenever a meal was served, when the yard was swept clean, or when something needed to be done. My dead child had been more visible to me than my living mother.

"No tears," she said, shaking her ladle at me.

———

The construction of our new house began and I could continually hear the sounds of hammering wood and cutting stone. Simon planned to build a house of several rooms and dry-stone basalt walls. There would be a thatched roof and few windows, except by the fireplace and the scullery. My husband wanted to erect an upper chamber for my weaving, although I had not returned to the loom since my mother arrived. The floor would be of black basalt cobblestone, as would be the courtyard.

For many months, Simon abandoned all endeavors for the singular task of building our house, showing a religious devotion to every stone and brick. The fishing enterprise was left to the management of Andrew and the Zebedee brothers. Between John's customer expansion, James's training of hired fishermen and Andrew's meticulous bookkeeping, the partnership had become a large and reputable provider of fish. Village girls began flocking to these prosperous young bachelors. While Andrew and John preferred celibacy, James indulged in a number of flirtations after being spurned by his beloved shepherdess. The colossus spun for himself somewhat of a reputation as a rake.

Old Salome, wife of Zebedee, alternated between caring for an ailing husband and worrying about her wayward son, James. Unable to confide in John, she sought me for companionship. I listened to her while she baked, kneading the dough and sprinkling yeast. James, the rough-hewn son, was the one who fell and bruised himself as a child, causing her constant apprehension. The younger son, so delicately formed, was much surer in his footing even as an adolescent. John had found his way, albeit in solitude.

"James has always been restless," the old woman said, then sighed. Her hands were white with flour. "Not unlike your Simon."

Despite the truth in her comparison, I resented it. I feared Simon's ambition. Whenever he became fixated on a new venture, everything else became secondary. My mother had warned me of the frivolous way men loved. For men, love was only one ingredient in that great, boiling broth of their lives. For women, love was everything. We could live on the hope of love alone.

———

The new house was not yet completed when my mother fell ill. Her illness initially invisible, she complained of fatigue and lightness in her head. Then there was the wavering in her weaving, and the lack of spice in her usually savory cooking. One evening, I found her unconscious on the scullery floor, beside broken earthenware bowls. Her face was flushed and her body was hot as if she had lain upon coals.

Nothing could assuage the fever. For days, I doused cloths in cold water and applied them to her brow, to no avail. I rubbed the sap of aloe and fig juice on her forehead and her chest, but they only seemed to incense the burning in her flesh. I chopped radishes into translucent slivers and spooned them into her mouth, but she never responded. Even the rapha's flaxseed oil, the labor of heavy bartering, did not help. Her eyelids fluttered, but they did not open. She spoke in delirium, murmurings of one close to death.

We brought the rapha to her bedside, and he shook his head in resignation. Fevers that burn the length of three days were life threatening, he intimated. Few survived. Indeed, upon touching my mother, it seemed that she was boiling from within. He pricked her with a long needle, but even bloodletting did not diminish the fever.

The rabbi insisted that she suffered from the wrath of God; such an affliction could only be the result of sin. He encouraged us to fast, to seek redemption with God in her stead. So Simon and I fasted. For three days and three nights, we abstained from food and drink. We sent a message to Andrew, who was in Jerusalem delivering fish, to visit the Temple in our stead. We smeared ashes upon our brows and donned the sackcloth appropriate for rites of denial. We knelt in penitence before the Lord until our knees were sore. Simon brought offerings of wine and grain to the synagogue, and rendered the proper sacrifices. I imagined him slaying a newly born lamb, its eyes moist from awakening. I imagined him cleaning the blood and dressing the lamb, placing it on the altar of burnt offerings in the heart of the synagogue.

The fever continued to consume my mother. A heaviness began to settle in my breast as I stroked the bloated texture of her skin and listened to her soft, rasping breath. I took her hand and her burning fingers twitched slightly. My childhood prayers fell from my lips, their repetition comforting because I had nothing else to say:

"Lord, smite me for the sins of my ancestors. Spare my mother."

My prayers continued on the Sabbath, the seventh day of her illness. I saw the synagogue from a distance, proud limestone that seemed newly fashioned on cloudless days. I walked gingerly to the site of worship, hand in hand with Simon. I was trembling after several days of fasting, my throat parched from prayer. Simon's strong arm guided me and his nearness lent me strength. I reminded him that I was to walk six paces behind as a proper wife should. He had insisted on walking abreast and I was glad his stubborn will had overcome mine.

We parted at the entrance steps, where vestiges of black basalt had become visible at the white corners. Simon proceeded to the front of the synagogue to join the men, while I lingered in the back among the women. It was the Sabbath and a crowd had congregated in the synagogue. Silks and frankincense of the rich mixed with coarse wool and deep musk of poorer folk. This was the rare occasion when all women occupied the same space, although the rich always stood at the front. Wedging myself behind a cobbler's wife and a merchant's daughter, I peeked through the throng of bodies.

I caught sight of a familiar back—a tall man attired in a peasant's garments. He held his head high and he moved with swift movements that suggested youth. He stood in the center of courtyard, and the gravel around him appeared so white it seemed to be glowing. All shuffling ceased as he spoke.

Then I heard the voice. It was a simple voice, the voice of a working man, yet it commanded with the awe of an orator. It was a voice I had heard before, twilight rising over the desert.

He turned his face. It was Jesus.

Without warning, the rancid smell of tombs filled the air. The crowed parted to reveal a dark creature crawling on all fours. I thought it was a beast, but then its body angled upright and I saw with a shock that it was a man. His face was hairy and so matted with dirt I could not tell where earth ended and skin began. He was cross-eyed, vermillion pupils staring angrily in multiple directions. Upon seeing Jesus, he shook convulsively and cackled.

"Ha! What have you to do with us, Jesus of Nazareth? Have you come to destroy us? I know who you are—the Holy One of God!"

Jesus took a step forward and looked at the madman. He cowered under the intensity of my friend's gaze, uttering unholy cries. The shrieking grew louder, reverberating in the courtyard, a demonic symphony of high and low-pitched voices.

Then Jesus touched the madman's forehead. "Be quiet!" he rebuked. "Come out of him!"

The cursed man threw himself to the floor, scratching and tearing his clothes. He swung his head like a pendulum, trying to overcome an unseen force pulling him apart. His body twisted in strange contortions, bending his legs backward and crumpling his arms; I feared his bones might break. He bared fangs, gnashing his teeth like a hound, and howled mournfully. Then the voices merged into one slow, sonorous cry. Blood seeped into his spittle, and his mouth foamed. Then he stilled.

An hour seemed to have passed. No one in the crowd stirred; all eyes were fixed on the madman. He sat up slowly and looked about him, his eyes focusing on the carpenter clad in a white linen robe. He stared at his hands with wonder, moving his appendages with a sense of liberation. Then he recognized the synagogue, and the assembly of worshippers attired for the Sabbath. He groped about his body, attempting to cover his nakedness, as he had torn off all but his loincloth. Shame registered on his face.

Without a word, Jesus untied his cloak and dropped it about the naked man's shoulders. The man wiped his brow, face, and neck clean as he wrapped the garment around his body. My friend extended his hand and the man grasped it without hesitation, allowing Jesus to pull him to his feet. He tottered, his footsteps unsteady, and he clung to Jesus to maintain his balance. Abruptly, he fell to his knees and praised Jesus.

The crowd began to chatter among themselves and pointed at Jesus of Nazareth. A few shook their heads, confounded at the spectacle. Some were still dazed by what they had seen. The merchant's daughter turned to her mother, jingling her gold-mounted ears. Accustomed to commanding attention, her voice rang higher than the rest: "What is there about his word? For with authority and power he commands the unclean spirits, and they come out." She urged her mother to take another look at Jesus, waving her garnished fingers in his direction.

He was gone.

———

I waited for Simon at the outer gate of the synagogue, as I usually did on the Sabbath. I looked forward to these moments, when we shared the silence and I could observe his wide, sloping back without being hurried. We did not need to be burdened by work, or by the world's demands. We could listen to the idiosyncrasies of one another's footsteps and I would walk briskly to keep up with my husband.

Today I wanted to talk to him about Jesus.

Simon, though, did not come. Villagers walked past me, question marks in their eyes. Minutes passed and I decided to go home. I could not loiter; my mother needed attending. At the entrance to our courtyard, I saw Simon entering. He was not alone.

Jesus was with him.

My husband had not seen me approaching, but Jesus beckoned me to come forth. I took a few steps forward into the light of the courtyard. When Simon saw me, he brightened and placed his hand on my arm. The pressure felt firm and reassuring.

"Teacher will see Mother and examine her ailment," Simon said. He turned to Jesus. "Teacher, you remember my wife."

I lowered my head as Simon drew me toward Jesus.

"Look at me, my friend," Jesus said.

I lifted my head. Jesus had changed. Gone was the questioning younger-looking man who had traveled with us. He appeared older, his skin was tanned, and he stood with authority. I remembered Andrew's words: the One who would bring salvation. Yet the expression in his eyes remained the same. That light, translucent as honey, was ever steady.

"Do you believe I can heal your mother?" Jesus asked.

I remained silent. Except for Simon and Andrew, few men ever asked for my opinion or my beliefs. My eyes sought out my husband's, and he smiled in reply.

I swallowed so my voice would not come out squeaky. "I believe in the miracle my eyes have witnessed."

I thought I saw a flicker of approval cross Jesus's face.

Simon, though, grew impatient: "Teacher, this way. Our mother will not last much longer."

I looked up and Simon motioned toward the door, shaking his head slightly at me.

Jesus seemed unhurried. He addressed Simon, but he scrutinized me. "Do not fret, my friends. Your mother will soon be well."

Simon led the way to my mother's bedchamber, a shuttered room where the shadows of dusk gathered. It was the farthest room from the front door and where the thatched roof was thickest. In the summertime, it was the coolest chamber in the house. In the wintertime, it garnered the most warmth. My mother lay motionless on the bed. Simon put his hand to her forehead and withdrew it quickly. I started toward the water basin, but my husband's arm restrained me.

Jesus stood over my mother's bed and placed his hands on both sides of her head, his long fingers spreading over her temples like a caress. Wisps of her hair fell through his fingers. He began to rebuke the fever, gently as though rebuking a child.

My mother stirred. She later told me that at his touch, a delicious cooling passed into her body. In the moment, I could sense the alleviation of fever, lifting into a raging cloud above her. The heat in the room suddenly felt oppressive. Sweat collected on my brow, and I saw that Simon's forehead glistened as well.

My mother opened one eye and then the other, the brilliance of lapis lazuli. She blinked and sat up with a jolt. Perplexed, she eyed Jesus and then looked back and forth from me to Simon. She straightened her tunic, frowning at the wrinkles. Then she clasped her hands together with some agitation.

"We have a guest," Mother said. "My children, you have forgotten your manners."

She swung her legs over the bed and moved to the scullery with the determination of a woman preparing a feast. I followed her, my eyes wide. Simon stood there; his mouth fell open.

In the scullery, my mother was always a magician. She pounded, chopped, and mixed ingredients in raw juices, bringing forth creations that made my mouth water. I would serve as her acolyte, slicing the meat, crushing the berries, and removing seeds from the fruits she most commonly used to spice her meals. Simon often remarked that I should have inherited my mother's flair for cooking along with her eyes.

That day, she cooked with a passion. We had two kinds of fish on hand: musht and sardines. The musht was fried and spiced with lemon juice; steamed sardines were sprinkled with salt. There were fresh dates, olives, and barley bread. She served the good wine, usually reserved for weddings and celebrations of birth.

The feast lasted hours. My mother and I scurried back and forth from the scullery to the table. Simon and Jesus were absorbed in conversation, their voices low and passionate. Simon leaned forward to better hear what Jesus was saying. I was surprised to see that Simon listened more than he talked. I tried to sit at Jesus's feet to listen, but my husband waved me away by requesting more food and drink.

After several cups of wine, Simon grew boisterous and flustered. He would begin to stutter soon, and so I brought a jug of cool water to ease his throat. Jesus was jovial, and I felt his presence behind me as I refilled his goblet. He seemed to be waiting.

I cleared my throat nervously. "Teacher—"

At the moment I began to speak, Simon toppled onto the table, red faced and unconscious. His goblet clanked against the floor and my mother rushed from the scullery at the sound. My cheeks burned with embarrassment. Simon was known for his inability to hold his liquor, despite his enthusiasm for the bottle. I apologized to Jesus while I propped Simon on my shoulder and ushered him to bed. A twinge of regret swept over me as I hurried about my wifely duties and avoided meeting Jesus's eyes. The chance to ask him was lost.

CHAPTER IX

"Simon?"

I roamed the shores of Capernaum, searching for my husband. Since the arrival of Jesus, we had entered a precarious season with no fish. The winds of the Great Sea had not favored us. Storms had interrupted the spawning of the musht and the river fish. Expeditions returned bereft of catch, and even the neighboring coastal villages of Magdala and Bethsaida reported a scarcity of fish. The village elders grew worried at the multitude of industries affected: fresh fish, salted fish, fish sauce, fish oil. Fish was the currency of Capernaum. Traders often took the raw, succulent catch or renowned fish products of our market instead of gold, Roman coins, or even spices, despite the universal fondness for coriander and cumin in these parts. Fish was the throbbing pulse of our village, connecting houses and families and loyalties. Our men smelled of fish, the pungent and repulsive odor we wives scrubbed fervently with lemon and loofah to remove. Fish was our identity, for what is a fisherman and fisherwoman without fish? Aimless, soulless, childless. Without fish, we could not survive.

Simon had taken to nocturnal fishing far from shore,

as his days were filled with the extraordinary doings of Jesus and interminable crowds seeking relief from the monotony and depravities of the human condition. Only in the dark, unbidden hours of the twilight could my husband and his partners pursue their destiny of being fishermen unperturbed. I worried about him. Simon's excursions into the deep waters every night left him exhausted in the morning, blank, glassy-eyed, and reticent. He kept me uninformed about their progress; I knew by his dejection they returned empty-handed. He brightened only in the presence of Jesus, casting off sleep privation at the carpenter's ingenious storytelling. He avoided me at daylight and I lay alone on my pallet at night, eschewing slumber while his strenuous and heroic attempts at fishing yielded nothing. I began to fear he would drown, his fatigue likened to inebriation, and opaque, unfriendly skies confounding him.

"Simon?" I called.

I circled the fishing dock, and saw the boats anchored at the landing, forlorn wooden shells without men. The waning moon gave way to the first flickering of dawn, and dark, writhing figures were visible on the far end of the beach. I ran toward them in the blackness, slipping on loose dry sand, squinting hard so my eyes teared profusely and I felt a blind fool, stumbling toward perhaps a band of thieves. Then I heard the panting and punctuated breathing, ragged, raspy breaths that could only be Simon's. The light intensified and I saw them lying on the shore, naked from the waist up and glistening like wet seals, flesh golden under the sun, chests heaving with effort. James the colossus was sprawled across the others, his great bulk obscuring the diminutive, fine-featured John who lay in a fetal position. Andrew's face was buried in his hands, body trembling and soft, shuddering sobs emanated from him. Unlike the others, my husband's eyes were open, staring into a great void, lips slightly ajar. His face was haggard, and his leathery skin was etched with more lines, culminating in three abject horizontals by his eyes. Beside him were the nets, conspicuously flat, dampened by the foaming waves that continued to lick their feet.

I untied my water pouch and put it to his lips. "Simon, darling, you seem ill. You are pushing yourself too hard. All the fishing towns are experiencing this drought. If there are no fish—"

"There are fish."

My husband stiffened and he gripped my wrist with such force in his choler that I could not feel my fingers. I could barely whisper. "Then why are the nets not full?"

I regretted it the moment I spoke.

Simon's eyes narrowed. "The fish eluded us. All of us. They swam with such speed that they broke through our nets. As if they were demons. As if there is a curse."

That was all he would say to me. He stood up shakily, cursing and muttering to himself coarse obscenities I had rarely heard him use. The others followed his lead, clutching the nets as they brushed the sand off their bodies, and in the twinkling of sunrise, I saw jagged holes in the nets, spaces of nothing once held together by a mesh, a web fraying at its ends.

———

The fish shortage continued and Capernaum began to grow desperate. Simon shunned me, saying he could not in good conscience lay with his wife until the village's livelihood was restored. Fishing excursions became constant, as the fishermen spent every waking moment scouring for fish, becoming evasive phantoms, as it had been weeks since we tasted fish. I found solace in Jesus. I learned to anticipate his measured footsteps, so unlike the halting stride of my husband. He delighted in the simple staple of bread and mashed chickpeas to quell his hunger, and for his thirst, barley beer. We could not afford to serve him wine any longer, nor did he mind. Honey cakes brought about a childlike joy in him, and he delighted in the smells of cedar and olive wood, the aromas of Egypt. I asked him about Nazareth, his home, and he laughed; as a carpenter, he said, he was invariably covered in sawdust and did not remember the scent of anything else.

One morning, old Salome sent for me. The sweetness of ripening figs laced the air, and she snorted at my pleasantries, being less concerned with ripening fruits than ripening women. I knew that tone; her cryptic manner of summoning me aroused my suspicion and together we hustled to her desired destination, the house of a farmer known for his talent cultivating pomegranates, dates, and melons. He was also the widowed father of a young girl, a timid, guileless thing who lagged behind the women at the synagogue.

We had scarcely crossed the threshold when the stout farmer drew us into the inner alcove of his abode and unequivocally demanded James the son of Zebedee must marry his daughter.

Old Salome feigned ignorance. "Why should James, who could have his pick of any girl in the village, marry a wisp of a girl whose moon blood has broken only once or twice? She is not yet fifteen."

The farmer flinched at this vulgar talk, as the mysteries of women were kept to women, and he sent for the girl.

"You should see for yourselves," he said, running his hand through his unkempt hair.

I noticed he smelled of drink and his eyes were bloodshot. The girl entered, eyes modestly downcast and heavily veiled even in her own house, and her father closed the curtains, preventing the thinnest sliver of light. She approached as he held a candle to her, and at his instruction, removed her thick woolen mantle and stood clad only in her linen tunic. The pronounced curvature of her belly was unmistakable. The farmer's daughter was with child.

"How long has it been?" Old Salome asked, tender

despite her annoyance.

"Three months," the girl replied. Her nose and cheeks were red; it was clear she had been weeping for many days. "I was at the market fair, when the almond blossoms were in full flower. I was so pleased to be noticed by James. He had bought a melon and crushed it open with his bare hands, sharing with me the pulp and offering me young goat's milk. He clasped my fingers in his and led me to a pasture." Crestfallen, the girl stopped, biting her lip in shame.

"You gave yourself to him willingly." Old Salome's voice was shrill.

"Yes," the girl blurted out before her father could stop her.

"My son did not make you any promises?"

The girl shook her head, looking down.

Old Salome gave me a sidelong glance. She cleared her throat. "My son will not marry you. I shall not embrace a daughter who is so easily led astray."

The farmer clenched his fists.The girl's bottom lip quivered, and she appeared like a cornered animal, a fearful expression in her eyes.

"But I understand the plight of a woman," old Salome said. "James is partly to blame for tempting you." She handed the girl a heavy purse and a sack bulging with provisions. She spoke slowly and deliberately, eyeing the farmer. "This is for the journey south. You shall stay with my cousin in Jerusalem until you have the child. Then you shall leave the newborn on the doorstep of the Great Temple. You may return to Capernaum after the Passover feast. You shall speak of this to no one."

The farmer growled. "No! My daughter is disgraced enough! I will take this to the judgment of the elders." The corpulent farmer banged his fists on the table so the goblets rattled, eyes blazing.

Old Salome simply frowned and shook her head. "That would be unwise, sir. What can you hope to gain from public humiliation? James behaved as all men behave. It is your daughter who will be branded a harlot. Any chance of an honorable marriage will be ruined."

The girl seemed to gain a measure of composure. She placed a thin hand on her father's portly shoulder. "Father, I will do as she asks. I will disappear. It is only for one season."

The farmer collapsed into a seat. We took our leave, hesitating as Zebedee's wife gave the farmer's house a final glance.

———

The village was in the throes of celebration when we returned. Fish, prodigious amounts of fish, were piled high at the dock, and the stench of raw fish was inevitably welcome after months of absence. Simon, Andrew, and the sons of Zebedee were the toast of the festivities, delivering fish in abundance, delivering Capernaum from certain ruin. Wine skins were filled and drained, spirits rising higher and higher as the intoxication ran rampant after months of restraint. Rumors also abounded that Jesus of Nazareth was good for business; his mere presence would make one prosper and his blessing would bring riches.

I came down to the fishing dock to catch a glimpse of the men, and saw Andrew mending the damaged seines, cleaning the fine linen mesh nets of seaweed and scales abandoned when fish were tossed too quickly onto shore. A few hired fishermen mirrored the process, scraping and tightening, and stretching the nets out to dry. The moistened mesh glinted in the sunlight, and they tied small stones to the bottom, reattaching the weights that were loose. Andrew worked in unison with the hired men, but the others were nowhere to be seen.

"Where is Simon?" I asked. "And Jesus?"

Andrew heard the inflection in my voice, the gasp I tried to suppress between the two names, and he looked at me quizzically.

"They are at the celebration."

"Why are you not with them?"

Andrew gestured toward the dock. "These nets must be cleaned or the mesh will rot and disintegrate. The boats must be repaired after the excursion this morning. The wood has splintered under the weight of so many fish, and had we not been close to shore, we would have sunk the boat."

"The excursion this morning…" I let the last syllable rest upon my tongue.

153

Andrew looked at the rock in his hands, inextricably tied to the wet, flaxen fibers, and then back at me. Then he nodded. "Last night was a sleepless night for all of us. We cast our nets far and wide in the sea. We rowed into the deep waters, treacherous in a storm, and indeed it rumbled with the hunger we felt in our own stomachs, the hunger of men to eat fish, creatures with blood and flesh that satisfy the raw desire of our teeth. Try as we might, our nets stayed empty. Bleary-eyed and exhausted, we rowed back to shore at dawn.

"Jesus was waiting at the shore. He waved and seemed fresh, as if the morning bloomed behind him. I envied the slumber from which he must have awoken. The boat had barely touched the dock when Jesus jumped onto the deck, both hands on the stern and told us to go back.

"James was the first to protest: 'The sea is barren and there is nothing for us to catch.' James turned on his heel and proceeded to stalk off the boat before Jesus stood squarely in his path and looked at him. I pleaded with him, 'Teacher, please, we have done everything we can and we are tired.' Jesus bent down and clutched the nets before he turned his attention to Simon. 'Go back,' he repeated. 'Put out into the deep water and lower your nets for a catch.'

"Simon glanced nervously at the two boats following us. 'Teacher, with not one, but three boats we have been scouring these waters for weeks. We have worked hard all night and have caught nothing.' Jesus gazed at Simon and

I hoped my brother would decide prudently. James's fists were clenched. John looked pallid with exhaustion. The hired laborers had a mutinous gleam in their eyes. Simon sighed and bowed his head towards Jesus. 'At your command, I will lower the nets.'

"We began to row back into the deep waters, the dark void of the night opening into a somber glow that was dawn. I saw our partners' discontent, the hired fishermen's grudging obedience, and my own hands raw from casting and pulling in the nets all night, repetition and dampness that had stiffened my fingers. I do not know what Simon saw. Maybe he was afraid of disappointing Jesus. He seemed moved by the conviction of a carpenter who had likely never tried to fish.

"The sky grew dim, and the clouds became ribbons of light breaking the monotony of sunrise as we approached the deep waters. The Zebedee brothers and I flung the nets out halfheartedly, for experience had taught us our thorough sweep of the deep water would have already uncovered fish if there were any to find. I yawned with one hand and held the net with the other, my fingers fluttering in the openings of the mesh.

"Then I felt it: pain. My hand caught in the insistent pull of the net toward the watery depths, heavier and heavier, the struggling net only going down, as though with a heavy weight. I threw my other hand toward the net and saw James and John hauling in this wild mesh that had a life of its own, surprise registering on their faces before determination replaced it. Their sinewy arms tense, muscles bulging, and their faces red. Simon was perspiring profusely and we were united in this fight, against the plunging net that contained treasures within. The hired men yelped in delight as they pulled onward against the weight, James cursing and Simon shouting.

"We pulled and pulled, and then we could see the fish, desperately swimming in the congested waters against each other, layered like large silvery coins, the net closing on them. The pattering of their fins was a drumming in my ears, an impending victory as the sound grew louder and louder. As we hauled the net out of the sea, for an instant we saw it shoot into the sky and then it fell onto the deck, along with all of us, a tumble of men and arms and legs and fish. Peals of laughter rippled across all three boats, and we could see the great mass of leaping fish, iridescent in the rising sun.

"'Again!' Jesus urged, and there was no question as to whose authority we obeyed. It was as if the fish followed us, clambering into the nets of their own accord. No sooner had the nets touched the sea than they would be filled to the brim with wriggling scales and fins. Again and again until it was threefold, sixfold, tenfold the yield of the first catch, boats creaking under the weight, the stench of fish and salt permeating our breath, the smells of men and musht mixed until fish and fishermen were the same. Jesus cheered us on, amber eyes twinkling and hearty laugh booming as the boat ambled from side to side, water

156

sloshing at our ankles. We were sinking!

"*We are sinking, we are sinking!* The words reverberated in my head and I do not know when I shouted, but James shrieked and began throwing fish overboard. John panicked and froze like a beam of wood. The hired fishermen began scooping out water with their cupped hands. Simon did not flinch. Indeed, I do not think he saw the danger. He collapsed to his knees before Jesus, his head lowered. There were shimmers on the corners of his eyes that might have been tears. 'I doubted you,' he said."

Andrew shook his head. "I have never seen Simon humbled. He has never genuflected before any man or woman, bowing his head like a servant. There he was, prostrate at the feet of Jesus. 'Depart from me, Lord, for I am a sinful man,' he whispered at first, and then louder and louder until it overpowered the commotion on the boat, a mantra as if he wished to undo some curse he placed upon himself. He beat his head with his fist, and then his heart, pounding himself with the very knowledge of his own inadequacy. Jesus pulled Simon's hands away and straightened his fingers. He touched Simon's forehead, reddened by his self-chastisement. 'Do not be afraid,' Jesus said. 'From now on, you will be a fisher of men.' And Simon let out an astonished wail, like a child's."

———

I sought Simon at the celebration, my old longing for him

reawakened. I found him bright-eyed and boisterous, the fretting furrow on his brow thankfully erased. We embraced without words, and found ourselves in our bedchamber, my head resting besides his, hands intertwined. We lay together as husband and wife. He traced his fingers against mine, lauding their length. Then he sighed.

"These hands have worked hard."

I laughed, "These hands are strong."

"I know," my husband nodded. "If anything were to happen to me, if somehow I had to leave you…I know these hands are capable. You will survive."

I sat up. "I would not want to survive. I would rather be by your side."

Simon did not answer. Instead, he pulled himself straighter and said, "Show me what else these talented hands can do. Let me see you spin."

I raised an eyebrow. "Spinning is women's work. You have never been interested before."

"I am curious about it now. Show me."

I climbed off the pallet and pulled the distaff, a long rod of acacia wood made from the shittah tree. I could almost smell the deserts of Sinai, where the shittah trees grew. I chose wool over flax, coarse animal fibers that were more tangible than the soft, smooth consistency of the flax plant.

Then I attached an unruly mass of wool on the distaff, large and billowing, thick like feathers upon the slender pole. I pulled several filaments of wool, straightening them, and then hooked them onto the spindle. The spindle was a splinter of bone that was sharpened at one end and attached with a heavy whorl, a small, circular bronze plate. With my right hand, I spun the spindle and the fibers twisted into a coarse string, held down by the weight of the whorl. Spinning again, the string tightened into yarn and I released more flax from the distaff with my left hand. It was a rhythmic, continuous motion. Slowly and deliberately, wild tendrils of wool were transformed into austere thread, bringing order from chaos.

My husband stared, fascinated by this rotation, the shaping of yarn from formless fleece.

He reached out with an odd sense of longing. Gingerly, my hands guided him along the distaff, the yarn, the spindle, the whorl. His calloused fingers, so used to hauling fishing nets, were clumsy. The spinning stopped.

"Simon, you have the dexterity of a bull," I chuckled.

He seemed annoyed. I placed his hand on the distaff behind the swirls of unspun wool.

"Hold it here. Like that."

I spun the spindle to demonstrate for him.

"Do not use too much force. Stronger is not better."

He tried again, but the spindle was stubborn under his guidance. It kept twisting and tangling the newly formed yarn in a hopeless mess.

"I give up," he muttered in frustration.

"You must be patient. Here."

I anchored the distaff in the hearth, and then I focused his right hand on pulling the yarn and his left hand on spinning the spindle. He followed my example, pulling when I pulled. I smiled as I thought how often he had taught me things through the years, even before marriage. He continued the rhythm, releasing and spinning. When he saw how the filaments were transforming, Simon became excited. He spun intently, fashioning the wool into yarn. His eyes acquired a vehemence as he began spinning faster, an impatience ruling his ethic, and the spindle wobbled dangerously. The fibers came out partly wrapped and partly loose, a poor bond in the yarn.

"Simon, you are spinning too quickly."

He seemed to forget that my hands were still trapped within his, my fingers on the spindle. His digits were becoming sweaty and feverish, spinning with abandon. Spindles had been broken by less force. I extended my thumb to stop the spindle, and my skin caught the tip.

The spinning stopped. Distaff and spindle dropped.

My thumb was pricked.

Blood.

The wound was peripheral, but I bled more than expected. Small segments of the yarn were scarlet as if they had been dipped in cochineal, the red dye made of crushed insects. Even the fleece on the distaff was darkened in spots by the blood.

Simon jolted, as if coming out of a trance. He paled at my bleeding finger and hastened to find the nearest bandage, a fine indigo linen that was my most prized headscarf, and wrapped my injured appendage with it.

"It doesn't hurt much," I assured him. I retrieved the fallen spindle. "You are making progress. Keep spinning."

My husband still looked horrified, but he took the spindle. He hooked a few strands of wool, and the spindle began rotating again. He looked intently at the scarlet splattered wool and the stained yarn and seemed mesmerized by the spindle, as if he saw visions in the moving whorl. As I closed my eyes to sleep, Simon was still gazing at the spindle and the vacillating yarn.

————

Simon was gone.

He left the spindle, distaff, and whorl on the floor. My eyes searched for the yarn, any evidence of Simon's handiwork, but found nothing.

I did not want to search for Simon. I was afraid of what I may discover.

I began to wait. I set up the loom, tightening the threads to unbaked clay weights. Standing upright, I stretched parallel threads across the warp, and then aligned the weft to construct right angles. I shuttled the heddle bar back and forth, watching a tapestry form.

I wove and wove. I found solace in the loom's shuttling motion, despite the pain in my bandaged hand. I did not want to think about Simon. Instead, I thought of Jesus. I imagined the resplendent light behind his eyes, how he listened attentively as if I was the only one who mattered. I remembered the warmth of his fingers. Fool was I to think his touch was reserved for me. I thought about the grimace that crossed his face after healing my mother, when the power went out of him. There were times when he was fatigued, but no one appeared to notice. There were times when he seemed sad.

The weft snapped. I had not knotted it tightly enough and the tapestry fell apart in my hands. It was a pitiful heap, so tangled that it was difficult to tell where one stranded ended and another began. I wondered if this was what had become of my story. I gathered it up quickly, fearing my mother's reprimand for wasting perfectly good yarn. I rushed down the ladder to dispose of my guilt into fire.

Flames began to lick the filaments when I heard pounding on my door. It glowed orange as if from rage, and then an inconsolable black. I held my breath and poked at the ashes. The hearth could hide all things. Still the pounding continued insistently. I opened the door.

It was old Salome. Her hair was disheveled, and she was panting. In she barged.

"Are they here?" she asked.

I did not understand.

"Where are my sons?"

"With Jesus."

"Jesus is gone. They are all gone."

I felt dizzy. It must have been sleep deprivation.

"Last night, not one of them came home!" she said. "I searched at the fishing dock; I went to the marketplace; I even went to the taverns, and no one has seen them."

"Last night," I said, "Jesus and the others ministered to a great crowd. They must be tired. Maybe they are sleeping somewhere. It wouldn't be the first time we found them camping out by the lake." I tried to make my voice reassuring, but Salome was not convinced.

"They are gone, I tell you, gone! To think he would steal my sons. After I gave him the seat of honor at my table…after I waited on him like a kinswoman!"

"Salome, please be reasonable—"

"I know when my sons have left me! You better watch that husband of yours."

I did not know how to answer her. I could not bear the thought of losing Simon.

I took a deep breath. Then a pungent smell filled my nostrils. It was the stink of mud, hay, and sheep.

The door was already open, swinging on its hinges. Thomas the shepherd was standing under my doorpost, his diminutive figure less overwhelming than his odor. His beard was curly and unkempt, even tinged red by the ochre he used to mark sheep. He seemed rather like a sheep himself, moist eyes and skittish movements. He nodded reverentially at us.

"Shalom. I am looking for Jesus of Nazareth. I heard

163

he was staying here."

"I'm also looking for Jesus," Salome growled. "He is a thief. He stole my sons."

Thomas looked bewildered.

"They have gone missing," I said.

Thomas wrung his staff in his hands. I could see gray streaks in his wild, reddish mane. "I...I saw him last night. He cured me of this terrible...Well, never mind."

Salome's eyes narrowed. "You saw them last night?"

The poor shepherd nodded. "Yes...Yes...Your sons were there." He looked at me. "Andrew the fisherman and your husband Simon were there too. Many sick people lined up to see him, thousands of men and women. Paralytics, cripples, even lepers. Demoniacs, fighting the ropes their kinsmen used to drag them to the sea. It smelled awful, all those diseases. I was afraid of catching something. If it was not for the boils that hurt so badly..."

He paused, then went on. "Jesus was there. He talked of prophecies. He said he was sent by the Father to anoint the sick, to preach to the poor, to heal the brokenhearted. He said many other things, but I forgot them. He touched everyone. All of them."

I leaned forward, "What happened next?"

"They were healed."

My lower lip trembled and I took a deep breath.

The shepherd's voice broke. "Then he spat into the ground and made mud. He rubbed it all over me and told me to wash. I ran to the sea, but the mud was already dried. My skin was caked and heavy. It came off in strips, like bark. The water felt cool and I felt warm inside. I felt my forearms and legs; they were smooth. They no longer hurt. My skin was whole!

"The entire crowd—everyone was laughing and splashing in the Sea of Galilee like children. The blind rubbed their eyes, squinting. The mute could talk. Even the crippled were running and casting their canes to the sand. When I turned around, Jesus was gone. The fishermen had disappeared too."

Thomas's eyes began to tear. "You do not understand how long I have suffered, how many medicine men I have seen. Do you know where I can find him? I need to thank him. Please."

I shook my head. I honestly wished he would leave. Shepherds were known to sleep with their sheep in the fields. Some even remarked that with sheep, there was no need for women. They smelled of dirt. Their clothes were rank, tattered, and unwashed. They were unclean, the lowliest of professions. No one wanted to receive them.

I said, "I do not know where they are."

Thomas did not reply. He just stared at me helplessly.

"My husband is also gone," I said.

As soon as I uttered the words, I knew it was true. Simon had left me. I grew cold, an icy chill entering my veins. My lungs felt constricted.

Salome wrinkled her nose, an odd glint in her eye. "You are not welcome here," she said to Thomas. "Get out, ruffian! Get your dirty self out of my neighbor's house!"

His eyes grew vacuous and even more watery.

"Out, I say!"

Salome held up a clay pot. Despite her age, she was far less frail than the slight shepherd. There was no station in life lower than a shepherd and Old Salome reminded him of where he stood. Even though it was my house, I did not stop her. Worry had made me callous.

Thomas stifled a cry; his face grew red with shame. He turned and ran, tripping over his shepherd's crook.

I wanted to kick myself for being unkind.

CHAPTER X

Much changed after my husband left. Tiberius Caesar appointed a new governor to the province of Judaea, a certain Pontius Pilate who had less taste for ruling than commanding an army. His predecessor Valerius Gratus had appointed Joseph Caiphas as head priest in Jerusalem, and he had left us to our own affairs. No one knew how Pilate would govern, although rumors of his fearsome temper became the talk of taverns. He was the fifth prefect in twenty years. It had been long since the lands of Judea, Samaria, and Idumea saw a Jewish king, even just in name.

Herod Antipas raised taxes to build a great amphitheater in Sepphoris. He envisioned gladiators and games, to win the favor of Rome. His brother Philip was campaigning for Tiberius to become king. His eldest brother Archelaus was swiftly deposed after falling out of the good graces of the Empire. Antipas collected taxes often, sparing no expense in constructing his magnificent coliseum. Tiberius Caesar was known to love the games.

Taxes were the least of our worries. When none of the partners returned to the fishing dock, the apprentices confiscated everything: boats, nets, fishing poles, and Andrew's ledgers. They claimed my husband owed them wages, and one prolific catch with Jesus did not compensate for the hapless fishing season. They also said he withheld wages to invest in the expansion into the fish processing industry, and they appropriated the new tools, salt and ingredients, all in which they asserted a share of ownership. The apprentices took the lumber Simon had purchased to build additional boats, and lanterns used during nightly fishing expeditions. Some fled to neighboring villages; others joined Hasar or larger fishing enterprises. Only one leaky boat was left, one that the apprentices did not bother to repair.

Old Salome and I pleaded our grievances to the aged Jesophat, most venerated among the village elders. As he spoke to me, the rabbi's mouth puckered as if he had bitten into a green persimmon. He maintained that he could not speak on behalf of a woman who disobeyed her father and who was abandoned by her own husband. "Such a woman…" Jesophat paused painfully. I feared the old village tongues were wagging in the marketplace.

Salome insisted that she too had been robbed, that the sons of Zebedee had been robbed. The rabbi shook his head furiously; his face grew red and contentious. The sons of Zebedee and their partner Simon were in debt. Jesophat and several of the village elders were among the creditors, and the accounts had to be settled at once. Despite the unfairness, Salome and I were forced to surrender all additional resources: salt and oils and equipment reserved to start the business of salting fish.

168

Jesophat and the elders also gained the writ of permission to build a fish-processing facility, for which Simon had invested a large proportion of savings to the Roman government. Our reserves were exhausted. Nearly everything of value was remitted to the elders or taken by the apprentices. The apprentices had fled and no one remained to stand trial.

———

I took up the yoke of my husband's station. The remaining boat, softened by years of battering water, was repaired and became my companion as I navigated for fish. The sea was temperamental, but I learned to live with it. I sat in the marketplace while the smell of fish permeated my hair, haggling over price and measure with my neighbors. My days were filled with perspiration, the sweat of a woman doing a man's work. My hands were sunburned raw like a naked crustacean and my lips cracked.

As I hauled fish from the nets, a stocky shadow caught the corner of my eye and my heart skipped in a familiar hope. Perhaps he came back to me. When I turned my head, the sanguine features of the neighboring fisherman came into view. He dragged his boat into the water, his back obscuring the sun.

Disappointment leaped into my throat. I wiped my lip; trickles of blood appeared moist upon my wrist. It had been over two months since he left and I could still hear his shuffling, hesitant footsteps on the beach. I turned again, half-expecting to see his impish grin beneath that prickly beard, and his contemplative eyes with a bad knack for staring, as if by gazing long enough he could ascertain truth.

Slowly, I attempted to lift the fish basket and trudged down the crowded thoroughfare, laden with bleating sheep and boisterous donkeys. Olive trees dotted the horizon; dunes of gold surround the sea. This was the land of my ancestors, the land of milk and honey. Vendors brushed past me, garments flapping and mixing with sweet aromas of ripened pomegranates, grapes, lemons, and figs. I quickened my pace, but I ended up dragging the fish. I was becoming accustomed to the heaviness of my load, yet the wicker fibers continued to bite into my fingers like needles.

"Ho, fisherwoman, what is the hurry?"

Joses the farmer pulled to my side atop a donkey pulling an oxcart overflowing with sacks of barley. The cart creaked ominously under the weight of its cargo. He had a pockmarked face and a rotund stature; he leaned forward with the pride of a lord.

"Can I give you a ride?"

I smiled and shook my head politely. He shifted his body closer to mine and I could smell spices of the field, wheat mingled with manure, emanating from his tunic.

"It is a long way to the market in this sweltering heat," he said with a conspiratorial grin. "Besides, it is not safe for a woman to walk alone. Times are tough. People are hungry."

I shrank from him, my hand involuntarily wandered to my throat, clasping the rose carved in olive wood.

"Thank you for your concern. I know my way well. Shalom."

I bowed my head and stared straight at the road, allowing the soft curtain of my mantle to conceal my face. The crowd was advancing down a hill, like a congregation of ants teeming toward a nest. I gripped my basket and ran to keep up with the other vendors. I heard the clacking of the farmer's wheels close on my heels.

"You are a proud one, are you not? Think you are too good for me? Your husband has run off, philandering across town expelling demons and such!"

His laughter reverberated long after he had driven off, leaving angry swirls of dust behind. I blinked instinctively and refused to cry, instead stumbling over pebbles in the footpath and landing on my side. The fish basket fell lopsided and the morning's catch was sprawled in the line of traffic. I caused an instant collision—small cages, a flurry of wings, and the terrible crunch of my fish trampled underfoot. An irate pigeon seller wagged her fingers at me, and threatened to take me to the constable. Beside her were two empty cages, latches undone and doors swinging on their hinges.

I picked up my basket and the remaining salable fish, smoothed my garments, and handed her a half shekel, one day's wage, for her losses. She grunted, and her withered face crinkled as she reached out with a gnarled hand. The money safely in her possession, she pursed her lips distastefully and mouthed something. Then she promptly turned her back on me, muttering about the kind of women that husbands leave, the curse they bring on their families and neighbors.

With my left knee skinned, I hobbled the rest of the way to the marketplace. There was little blood. As I settled into my customary stall in Market Square, I suddenly felt conspicuous. I sensed the watchful eyes of the vendors comb over my presence like a knife. My damp sleeves were rolled at the elbow and my skirts hitched above my ankles, dripping with ocean. My mantle had fallen away and my wild hair had taken shape with the wind. There was a burning in my cheeks, a flush perhaps.

I closed my eyes for a moment and imagined the wind embracing me.

———

My mother and I were baking bread when Salome burst in upon us, breathless. I was glad for old Salome's visits. After the departure of Jesus and my husband, the house seemed empty. No one visited us after that.

"Do you know the stories they are telling about you in the market?" she demanded. In her excitement, gray tendrils escaped her veil and flew about her head like mist.

I shook my head and placed the last loaves into the oven.

172

"That Simon wanted to divorce you. That you are barren, and your barrenness is the reason he left. Others say that you have committed adultery, and your husband could not bear to live with the shame. No right-minded husband would leave his wife and a prosperous business. You must have done something to drive him away."

I pursed my lips. "My husband left to follow Jesus."

"No use jutting your chin out at me. The two fools, my sons, are also following that wandering young rabbi."

"Why do they believe such things of my daughter?" my mother asked.

"Only young, unmarried fools follow the fanatics. Just last week, a caravan of them marched down to Jerusalem to protest Pilate putting up ensigns in the Holy City. All of the married men, young or not, stayed with their wives and children. Only Simon left, and he did not bother to provide for your future."

"He left us the fishing business," I replied defensively.

"Which those no-good apprentices stole from us. Mind you, I am not passing judgment. I know it is not your fault and I suffer from the same. Abandoning one's parents is no better than leaving one's wife. According to the Law, parents are to be honored, not cast aside. To think this Jesus is a great teacher of the Law."

I frowned. I did not like to hear his name in ridicule. "He is more than a teacher. He is a prophet."

"You too?" Salome laughed bitterly. "Well, because of this prophet, the entire village is questioning your honor."

I bowed my head, kneading the dough furiously.

"Your daughter needs to be mindful of her words and her conduct," old Salome said to my mother. "As a neighbor, I can only defend her name so many times. Nothing damages a woman more quickly than market talk."

My mother sighed long after old Salome left. I listened to her heavy breathing in silence—the deafening silence that followed us everywhere in this house. My mother worried. I saw how the lines of frustration broke the bronze plain of her forehead. I felt the weight of her anxiety, a disturbance in her blood that traveled to the irregular palpitating of her heart. My mother had a weak heart, although I never knew what made it weak.

"My daughter, Capernaum is a small village. Perhaps you should stay indoors and hire laborers, work behind our neighbors' scrutiny. It is imprudent to expose yourself after your husband's departure. To labor as a man, hauling the lines and nets…people will continue to talk."

"People are already talking."

"It will get worse."

"Amah, you cannot protect me from slandering tongues. Even if I stay in this house."

She looked at me with sad eyes. "I know, my daughter. At least your life is safe here. Out there, they can condemn you. Sometimes, they don't even wait for a gathering of the elders. Or a village trial. Sometimes, they act on their own."

I did not respond.

I did not tell her about the season of sparse catch, how the fish had not spawned, and about the thin, scraggly specimens we managed to swallow in our nets. I did not tell her of the threadbare sails. I did not tell her the shape of the boat, ancient in years as she, and the inevitable faltering of wood. I did not tell her of Simon's ambitious plan to expand the fishing business, monies the apprentices had pocketed, and the debt we had undertaken.

Perhaps she already knew.

———

In fishing villages like ours, lanterns were usually extinguished at night, as oil was costly. I spent many shekels on lamp oil since my husband left, and I mended his tunics late into the night. Needle and thread became my chief comfort in the hours before daylight. I held the soft wool in my fingers and it exuded a fishy scent, sweat mixed with the residue of the sea. I breathed it deeply. It was not pleasant, but it was the smell of my husband.

His spare sandals lay in a corner, as did his money pouch. His treasured mantle, which he wore only to the synagogue and on festivals, was folded beside the lopsided bed that he built for me. The rest of his clothes were piled in a wooden chest by the window. My ivory comb, which he used to untangle his beard on feast days, rested on the table. On the Sabbath, we had fought over whose hair would be smoothed first and Simon sometimes hid it from me. The comb sat in plain view now, and I left it where it was.

It was as if he was gone only for a moment. As if he would soon come back.

Then I saw it. A blade of flint, reserved for circumcision. Its edges were jagged and unused, the blood of Simon's son had grown cold before it was time to cut his foreskin. Our firstborn dead. I remembered my husband consulting the village elders for an illustrious name, and reviewing the family ledgers to ensure compatibility with generations past. Perhaps he had always known he would have a son. I remembered how the name had stiffened on his lips, unsaid, and his refusal to bestow that name. Bar Simon was a name born of my desperation. I began to wonder if Simon would return.

CHAPTER XI

Without warning, my belly began to swell. After Bar-Simon, I did not mark the passage of each new moon by carving lines on an olive branch, as many of the wives did. If the blood did come, I was not melancholy. I knew my womb was damaged, that life slipped from its tender curvatures and dissipated into the netherworld. I never thought I could be with child again.

It was after a ceremonial washing that I noticed the absence of my cycles. Menstruating women were kept away from the house of God, for they were unclean. After I dipped myself into the mikvah of old Salome and Zebedee, I realized I had attended the synagogue without fail for many weeks. I began to see the thickening of my abdomen, a fullness where I had been empty for so long. A child was growing inside of me.

I could not hide a smile as the rabbi told of the birth of the prophet Samuel on the next Sabbath. Although beloved of her husband, the pious Hannah was barren for many years. After copious weeping, she appealed to the Lord and made a promise to dedicate her son if she should ever have one. The Lord answered her prayer with a perfectly formed boy, Samuel, the seer of Israel. In the rumbling monotone of the Rabbi Jesophat, I heard music. I carried the seed of my husband deep within me, and Simon would always be with me.

"Wipe that smirk off your face," my mother whispered, nudging me.

I nodded. I lifted my skirts slowly so as not to be conspicuous, and I caressed my protruding tummy.

I did not suffer from nausea as I had with Bar Simon. Fishing occupied my days, and the work was somehow less tiresome. I rowed at the helm of the boat, humming as I waited for the nets to fill with fish. My luck had changed since the discovery of my pregnancy. Twice the boat was heavy with fish, jumping in the tangled nets and reflecting the sun along their scales like silver coins. It was musht, which fetched high prices at the marketplace.

My mother noted the change in my appetite. I was ravenous, devouring the bread, pottage, and figs she placed before me like a starving bird. No meat. Meat was a rarity in our home after Jesus and Simon departed. We could not have too much of the fish, as the market baskets were waiting and we had other debts to be paid. Nonetheless, I grinned at my good fortune and stroked my belly, throbbing with an infant soul.

Then I began to show. My woolen tunics were too thin to hide the bulge, and I required the longest mantles to cover my girth. My back grew sore, and my feet became too bloated to fit my sandals. I began to wear my husband's sandals, the coarse shoes of a working man, though Simon's feet had been smaller than most. It became harder for me to fish, and I endeavored to sit while the nets were sprung, hauling them up at the last minute.

———

"You have to leave Capernaum." My mother spoke quietly as we prepared pottage. Her voice held a warning, a gravity that rose above the gurgling of boiling water.

"Why?"

"I keep my eyes and ears open in the market, after the synagogue, during all religious gatherings. Anywhere people might talk. They are talking about you again. New rumors are swarming."

"Let them think as they please."

I lifted my chin as I sliced the roots for the stew. A handful of oats and grain would make enough pottage for a week. Olives were too valuable for a daily meal, and I placed them back into the oil-filled jars. I had no time for idle gossip.

My mother gripped my shoulders. "Daughter, I have indulged you long enough. I know you are happy, as happy as when Jesus was here. But you must not be blind. The elders are displeased. The neighbors are watching you. It is no secret you are with child."

"I am carrying Simon's child."

"That is not what they believe. Besides, your husband is not here to claim the child. You cannot protect the baby

179

by yourself."

"My husband will come back."

"Open your eyes, my darling. Simon will never come back. He was touched by the Son of God who has touched us all. He will follow Jesus to the ends of the earth. You must not fault him. Remember how he revived me." My mother sighed. "If your husband will not return, you must follow him. Take his path."

"Amah, be reasonable. I cannot possibly make such a journey in this condition."

"You be reasonable. Think of the child inside your womb. Your child will have no father. Your child will go hungry; fishing barely yields enough to feed two mouths these days. Your child will be scorned and slandered if you stay here. Your child will suffer."

"But," I said, "I do not even know where they are."

"Then you have not been listening to the news of Jesus. He goes from region to region performing miracles, healing the sick, and preaching the word of salvation. They say a small band of disciples follows Jesus wherever he goes. I heard he attended a wedding at Cana, where he changed water into wine. Six stone jars, about thirty gallons each, into the finest wine anyone could imagine.

"Then he was sighted in Nazareth, where the villagers threw him out of their synagogue. Last I heard, Jerusalem was in an uproar because of the commotion Jesus made in the Great Temple. He overturned the tables of the money-changers, dove sellers, and vendors of oxen and goats.

Using a whip made of cords, he lashed out at them saying, 'Take these out of here and stop making my Father's house a marketplace.' Jerusalem …" My mother fixed her gaze on me. "That is where Simon is."

I hesitated, then said, "Capernaum is my home."

My mother shook her head. "You wait and waste away here. You labor with the boats and nets, even though you are poorly suited for fishing. Your eyes are red in the mornings, and you cry through the night. Why do you stay?"

"The fishing enterprise, the work of Simon's life—he wanted to be his own master. I know it is not worth much now, but if I keep it going …" I trailed off. What else could I say?

"Do you not see? Your husband has abandoned it. They all have. Simon has found a new calling."

"What about you, Amah?"

"Your brothers will take me in. You must not worry about me."

I took a deep breath.

My mother laid her hand upon mine, her long fingers stiffened by years of work after she came under Simon's roof. I had wondered at this needless drudgery; certainly my brothers Levi and Reuben had servants at her disposal. Her embrace was the sole comfort that did not dwindle with time, temperament, or circumstance.

"I know you are afraid," she said. "Jerusalem is a long and arduous journey. But for the sake of your family and your child, you must go. Your life is no longer here. A wife belongs at her husband's side, serving him." She paused and stared into my eyes. "And for the sake of your soul, you need to follow Jesus."

I looked at her. "What? Amah, what do you mean?"

"I have seen the hunger in your eyes. You are writhing in hurts of the past. Your father, Bar-Simon, even Simon's departure. You need forgiveness and release from your own guilt. I have watched you swallow your questions, child, while your husband and his brother conversed with Jesus. You doubt your own worth to speak to him. They say that Jesus talked to Samaritans, forgave prostitutes and tax collectors, and even healed the slave of a Roman centurion."

She shook her head. "Do you not understand? Jesus offers forgiveness to all. Even to pagans. Even to women. Even to lepers. Faith renders you worthy, not your station."

Her eyes lifted toward the sky. She was not looking at me any longer. She began to mouth familiar words: "Blessed are those who are poor, for the kingdom of God is theirs. Blessed are those who are hungry, for they will be satisfied. Blessed are they who are now weeping, for they will laugh."

Then she looked at me again. "Go," she whispered. "Seek forgiveness. Seek a new life."

———

Unlike my bold, impetuous Simon, I could not leave the house we had built together. I could not embrace the vision of heaven without experiencing it. I lacked the faith to follow. In remembering Jesus, I trembled. I suddenly felt broken. A heavy pain struck my heart, pain from an old wound, and the weight of it was unbearable. The words rose to my lips and I spoke it for the first time. It was a question that I had longed to ask Jesus, but I could not ask in the throes of a crowd or within earshot of my husband.

Am I called to follow him?

I left when the world was still asleep. Day was breaking, a faint ribbon of light over the horizon. My mother had arranged passage for me with a traveling troupe of Parthian musicians and dancers who were passing through Capernaum on the way to Jerusalem. They readily accommodated me, and I saw my mother's cherished bangle glitter on the forearm of the eldest woman in the caravan.

They were pagans. Their language, their customs, and even their smells were alien to me, perfumes muskier than any Hebrew woman would dare entertain. Their skin was bronze; their almond eyes and eyebrows were perpetually decorated with kohl so they seemed rather hawk-like. These women laughed with abandon and sported uncovered heads, their dark, luxuriant hair billowing in the breeze.

They were dancers, highly skilled dancers from an

183

ancient school renowned in Susa and all of Parthia for their intoxicating movements. Roman nobles offered high sums for their performances, and only gold, not force, could sway them, as the Parthian Empire was not yet under the dominion of Rome. The caravan traversed many lands and mountains, pleasing Greek, Roman, and Jew alike. I could see the chests that held their gold were guarded by the watchful eyes of four Ethiopian giants. Thin musicians walked alongside the carts laden with instruments, which they valued more than any precious metal.

I did not speak their language; indeed, I did not speak unless spoken to. Zionna, the head dancer who accepted the bargain with my mother, spoke Latin, Greek, and a smattering of Aramaic. The other dancers murmured in Parthian, a thick and darkly spiced tongue, like cinnamon. They watched me as I watched them, a foreigner in their midst. I learned to sign for what I needed, and even those interchanges were few. I had never felt more alone.

The journey proved grueling, exacerbated by the arid desert air and oppressive heat of the sun beating down on us. My feet, bloated since the third month of my pregnancy, began to bleed against Simon's rough sandal straps. I had no salve to soak my blistered toes, and the boiling sun did little to ameliorate the pain. With my weight concentrated on my belly, I leaned backward to ease my sore back.

I trudged slowly at the end of the caravan. My own

sweat filtered into my eyes, burning, and for a moment, I thought I had gone blind. When I blinked, I had fallen behind the last donkeys that pulled the carts of instruments and the accompanying musicians. I ran to keep in stride, but I simply didn't have the strength.

"Wait! Wait!" I croaked. My voice was parched and I feared it did not carry far. The caravan kept moving farther away from me, leaving a whirl of dust behind. I slumped in exhaustion.

Then the caravan stopped. I saw a donkey galloping toward me, urged onward by its rider. It was Zionna. She whispered a few halting words to me—"Are ill?"—and I pointed frantically to my round belly and gestured that it was only to get bigger. The head dancer nodded with understanding, and I felt my knees buckling. The last I remembered was the evergreen of her eyes, the same hue as the emerald on my mother's bangle.

It was the rocking that awoke me, and I saw the swishing tail of a donkey as I opened my eyes. I was lying in a cart, surrounded by wooden flutes and small bells strung together like branches of hyacinth. There were also a number of drums and tambourines and stringed instruments that I did not recognize. They jostled whenever the wheels hit rocks in the path, and the musicians eyed the cart nervously. I rode in silence, save the tapping of the donkey's hooves and the occasional exclamation from a musician whenever the poor beast stumbled. On earlier pilgrimages to the Holy City, my kinsmen had filled the air with song and prayer and stories of Jacob or David or Samson among the Philistines. Never had it been so quiet. The absence of speech made me uneasy.

Scorching winds filled my ears and the warnings of my mother grated against me like sand. I stroked my swollen belly, knowing my neighbors would indeed brand the child a bastard. I was a coward. I did not have the courage to find my husband. I did not want to understand why Simon had left me. I did not want to face the plain truth: my husband had found something greater than our love. I could not accept that anything was greater than the love between us, a melding of two lives into one and from one, the rising of a new generation.

CHAPTER XII

The Parthian caravan stopped at several wealthy homes along the way to Jerusalem: in Cana, Shechem, and Sepphoris, where patrons had ordered performances for their lavish feasts. Bethany was the final city before our destination, an appointment at the grand house of the head scribe of Bethany. Nathaniel was known to advise the Sanhedrin on legal affairs, and he was one of the most venerated scholars in the whole of Judea. He resided in a palace of marble and granite, with many imported luxuries such as Grecian friezes on the floor, Egyptian tapestries, and wines from Rome.

It was a familiar engagement for the Parthian caravan. The musicians quickly assembled their instruments, the dancers donned their costumes, and I was given the role of crushing berries into juice that Zionna and her troupe used to redden their lips. Bangles and bracelets were arrayed at the proper provocative angle, and I polished the decorative knives used in the final sequence of their dance. I straightened the folds of their satin garments, and adorned their necks with ivory charms made from elephant tusks. Then I stood behind the curtains with the Ethiopian guards and watched.

The solitary note of a flute opened a melody that was soon accompanied by tinkling bells. The dancers appeared beneath a swathe of cerulean silk, the undulations of their bodies smooth as water. I had never seen gauze that transparent, clinging to every lithe movement. Tambourines raised, the dancers formed a circle around Zionna, who stretched her limber arms and elongated her body before the audience, a nymph praying to the gods. Slowly she spun, her fluttering robe allowing glimpses of her full bosom and bronzed midriff, while the others fanned about her in a symmetrical formation. For a moment, they collectively resembled an eagle with flapping wings, and Zionna was the soul of the creature, her dark eyes glittering with intelligence.

Faster she twirled until she appeared to be a divine opus of gold and turquoise, floating in their midst. Suddenly, she stopped and it seemed the world had stopped turning. Spectators lurched forward with anticipation. The other dancers encircled her again as Zionna stood, frozen in a beckoning gesture. Then she continued the dance, the music quickening to synchronize with her airy footsteps. Her cherry-colored lips were barely visible beneath her veil, and the slightest hint of a smile appeared. Her teeth flashed and I knew she was grinning. The dance was almost over.

At her cue, I slid two decorative knives to her across the floor. Blades in hand, the danger elicited spontaneous applause among the audience. Zionna became a warrior, slashing metaphorical enemies with long, bold strokes. The other dancers fled, scattering with the grace of leaves. At last, the battle was concluded and Zionna glided forward, twin swords forming a cross on her chest, and knelt as the music faded rhythmically. With the last note, Zionna paused dramatically and fell gracefully into her choreographed death.

The applause was astounding. Coins were thrown without caution. Showers of gold bombarded the dancers even before Zionna lifted herself from the final act. The musicians, dancers, Ethiopian bodyguards, and even I ran out to pick up the hard-earned fruits of labor. Nathaniel the head scholar congratulated the dance troupe, offering lodging before the caravan headed to the next metropolis. Zionna graciously declined the offer, insisting they had already made arrangements to stay in a well-frequented inn. Besides, she explained in her deep voice, it was not the troupe's custom to lodge in a patron's home. I saw Nathaniel turn angrily back to his seat on the mountain of silk cushions, his face blushing with thwarted desire. The interchange was in Greek, but his jovial friends translated to Hebrew among themselves and I found myself nodding in reverence of a pagan woman.

Jerusalem was near. I felt its presence in my bones, the calling of a holy city that existed in the heart of every Hebrew. My husband was near. Jesus was within reach. As I grew more excited, the fear of confronting my own demons also grew stronger. I began to see myself, a sinful woman cast off by her father and her husband, who caused the death of her son, shunned by her kinsfolk. Even as I stood on the firm grounds of Bethany, I felt myself falling into an infinite darkness. Cold enveloped my insides even though it was late in the month of Chevshan and the climate was warm and temperate. I was rootless on my own. I was nothing. If only I could see Simon again.

———

Jerusalem was in the throes of celebration when we arrived. Young men were drunk in the streets, red faced and exuberant from victory cheer. Loud music resounded from the taverns and brothels, filled with the persistent battering of drums. Dwindling smoke from recently extinguished campfires surrounded the palace of Herod in the capital, where the governor resided. A handful of Roman officers patrolled the vicinity. The brass effigy of Tiberius Caesar was nowhere to be seen.

The bazaars were teeming with crowds, no less than during the festivals when pilgrims saturated the marketplaces along their way to the Great Temple. It was not long after the Feast of Tabernacles. The caravan passed an olive merchant, hawking his bottles of fine oil to the highest bidder, and then stopped at the stall of a fruit vendor with baskets of figs. While the troupe bought provisions, I inquired about the state of Jerusalem.

The old vendor's eyes twinkled as she relayed the news. "Gotten our decency restored. That is what happened here. Even just days ago, graven images of the Romans desecrated our fair city, visible from every corner. Pilate allowed his soldiers to bring the cursed ensigns here, despite knowing the Laws of Moses. The Sanhedrin tried to reason with him, to no avail. Jews from every tribe, even as far as Samaria and Galilee, marched to protest the sacrilege. Finally, all of Jerusalem assembled outside the governor's house and demanded he remove the ensigns. We waited for five days. He deliberated and then refused, ordering his soldiers to surround us. Spears raised and arrows pointing, Pilate said he would kill us all if we did not submit. We were not afraid of death. We would rather die than desecrate the Law of Moses. We stood our ground proudly; even the young ones were not afraid."

The vendor paused dramatically. "Pilate removed the votive shields. The whole city has been celebrating since, especially the young men. It is very good for business, you know. This is a busy season for the prostitutes, and it grows busier by the day. The wine merchants have already emptied their cellars. Of course, I could find you some."

I lowered my voice: "Have you news of Jesus of Nazareth?"

She gave me a sidelong glance. "That madman?" The vendor shook her head. "He is bad for business."

"Do you know where he is?"

"If you know what is good for you, you do not want anything to do with him."

"Please, I need to find him."

191

"I have other customers to attend to."

I wanted to ask about his followers, but Zionna came up behind me with a few coins. The old crone snatched the money out of the dancer's hands and quickly turned to another woman inspecting figs. I bid farewell to Zionna. I thanked her. I would have liked to say more to her, but the Parthian caravan stood near. She put her hand on my arm and her gesture was oddly intimate, of one sister relating to another. She smiled and I noticed crinkles around her heavily lined eyes. She seemed almost old. Then I rushed into the throng to find the whereabouts of my husband and Jesus.

No one would tell me where to find Jesus of Nazareth. The sellers and tradesmen of Jerusalem regarded him as a bad omen. He had antagonized the mercantile class after remonstrating peddlers in the Great Temple, casting them out with such vehemence that many had feared for their lives. They had a litany of grievances against him: damaged goods, lost sales and opportunity costs, duress in the most commonly accepted channel of selling, namely the Temple. Most vendors shuddered when his name was mentioned; others told me to avoid him altogether. He was considered the very nemesis of commerce.

I had forgotten the chaos of the marketplace. I had forgotten about animals bleating their way to the sacrificial altars. I had forgotten about the trinkets and cosmetics and varieties of decadence, abundances of oil and spice. Pilgrims and natives crossed the thoroughfare without giving way, trampling on each other's toes. Bargaining resounded in myriad voices; price was discussed every which way and the clinking of coins was the most satisfactory reply. Bold men and flighty women laughed heartily together, holding empty wineskins between them. Crones with hooked noses relished in the latest stories, entertaining customers with juicy details. I listened for gossip. I strained my ears for the doings of a carpenter from Galilee.

I was so intent on finding him that I bumped headfirst into a tunic reeking of incense. I looked up. It was Adonijah, grandson of Jesophat of Capernaum. He was studying to become a scribe at the Great Temple. It had been several years since I had seen him in the rabbi's house before he left for Jerusalem.

"Adonijah!" I said.

I felt glad to see someone from home, although my countryman no longer resembled a Galilean. Adonijah had an air of erudition belonging to the higher echelons of learning. He appeared baffled. I pulled my mantle away from my cheek so that he would recognize me. During the journey, I had veiled my face to withstand the harsh sun and the biting desert winds. I told him my name.

He nodded and looked at me curiously. "Why are you here?"

"I am looking for my husband."

"Simon is in Jerusalem?"

"Yes."

"Why did you not wait at home? The Feast of Tabernacles is over. All the pilgrims are returning now. The delegation from Galilee has already departed."

I bit my lip. "I…I do not know if he is coming back."

"I see."

His eyes washed over me, resting upon the bulge that had grown so heavy. I wondered if he had heard the talk from Capernaum. Old Jesophat was notorious for circulating village news to distant kin, although his nephew was known more for his discretion than for love of idle gossip. I dropped my eyes and stared instead at tangerines in a nearby stall. Adonijah picked up the fruit, squeezing them to see if they were ripe.

"I will take these," he called to the vendor, tossing her a coin. He turned to me with a grin and handed me a tangerine. "You look famished."

I accepted his offering, peeled it, and bit into the fruit slowly. It was unexpectedly bitter. He watched me as I ate.

"Why is Simon in Jerusalem?"

I bit into a seed inadvertently and spit it out. I wiped the juice from my mouth with my sleeve and suddenly realized my mistake. It would become sticky. I no longer wished to discuss my husband.

"Can you tell me where to find Jesus of Nazareth?"

"What do you want with that heretic?" Adonijah said, then snickered.

"Please, it is important."

"He is not very popular in the Temple. He claims to be the Son of God."

"Where is he?" I cringed at the urgency in my voice.

Adonijah looked amused. "He is usually on the Mount of Olives, spinning blasphemies."

He pointed to the north of the Kidron Valley, the light of dusk congregating around the highest peak so that the sky appeared to be of pure gold. Rows of limestone houses glittered along the length of the mountain, like bracelets adorning the crown of God. I trembled at their sheer beauty.

"What is the quickest road to the Mount of Olives?"

"Come, I will take you there."

Adonijah grinned. I noticed for the first time that his teeth, like his linen robe, were splendidly white. He took me away from the bazaar through a footpath that bypassed the Great Temple into the hilly regions where the affluent built their homes. The sounds of the marketplace grew distant. The path was narrow and steep, crowded with vegetation that thrived in this arid climate, and with long twisted vines sporting enormous thorns perched on slim stems. Adonijah urged me in the upward direction, and warned that the Nazarene might well be gone if we continued this lagging pace.

The path reached a point of seclusion, as if the denizens of the city no longer cared to build among the thicket that sprung around upper ranges of the mountain, where trees were more companionable than people. Few travelers crossed this road, where it seemed remote from civilization even though it was mere miles from Temple and the great, churning crowd that never ceased to frequent such religious places in times of desperation. It grew more desolate, this interminable winding trail that persisted up the mountain, seeming to never end.

I heard Adonijah breathing heavily. Then he stopped and I fell forward with the suddenness of his halt. He threw himself on top of me, pulling my tunic up to my navel. I gritted my teeth, and when I turned my head, my left eyelid was scratched by gravel. My belly convulsed and I heard a ripping, but whether it was my clothes or my flesh I was not sure. I thought only of my baby as I scrambled away from him. Then he grabbed hold of my neck, and somehow ripped Simon's amulet away. I stiffened my body in resistance. He was so close, prying me open with my legs trapped beneath his. Out of my good eye, I saw in Adonijah's face the animal instinct that elicited the very worst in men.

"For shame! In the middle of the street!"

A rotund woman stood behind us, clinging to an earthenware jar as a shield, as if that was a physical barrier that separated her from sin. Remains of another jar littered the ground around her, evidently shattering when she came upon us in shock. She seemed a spinster by her look, with a distaste for the proximity between men and women, and a ready jealousy of pleasure. She eyed me suspiciously and her lower lip quivered, mouthing the words "fornication" at my wantonly exposed bosom.

Adonijah straightened. Though soiled, his white robes retained the station of a scribe of the Great Temple. His apology rendered him even more dashing, particularly to a woman who could not sustain the attention of most men. His voice was low and contrite, soothing velvet tones that Indian traders used to charm snakes. He bowed his head to the woman and offered to make reparations for her loss with a small pouch, heavy with coins. Then he pointed a finger at me. I bent my head as I retrieved the rose carved in olive wood.

———

I stood before the Sanhedrin. It was the lower tribunal, an arc of twenty-three men with thick beards and unforgiving eyes. The group comprised Sadducees, scribes, tribal elders, and Pharisees, appointed by High Priest Joseph Caiphas himself. The Great Sanhedrin, the highest court of justice in Israel, would not hear a common charge of adultery. Presiding in the high priest's stead was Annas, his father-in-law.

I was attired in mourning, as befitted the accused, and my left eye was too swollen to be open. The Temple was a vast configuration of labyrinthine chambers and hidden rooms, where the political power of Judea was truly exercised. Despite Roman intervention, the Sanhedrin was the all-abiding authority, the voice of God on earth. The chamber occupied by the Sanhedrin was stark and hollow, with a propensity for echoing. I heard whispers of the proceedings before the trial began. Adonijah had allies here, as the scribes were known to be fiercely protective of their own.

My accuser bowed before the Sanhedrin, with his hair slicked and garbed in immaculate white linen. Adonijah cleared his throat, and I saw the interchange of glances between the men. I saw their condemnation before any word was uttered. I lowered my head and trembled; my very heart seemed to be vibrating. There was no hope.

"This woman, by her very nature, is a sinner," Adonijah said. "Because of her disobedience, her name was excised from the family record and her father has renounced her. She married the fisherman Simon Bar-Jonah of Capernaum, proving herself a poor and promiscuous wife. The husband has abandoned her out of shame. See how she stands, unbalanced behind a wedge of flesh. I tell you, this woman is pregnant with a bastard!"

He paused, no doubt for effect. "Last night, this woman dared to desecrate a man of this Temple. She tried to seduce me, student to the great scribe Joshua of Jerusalem. In the pursuit of sin, this woman showed demonic strength. Thankfully, the Lord watched over me and I did not yield to her temptations. See the blood upon her brow, where we struggled. That is the living proof of her actions. She stands before you now, cloaked in modesty, to deceive you. Yet the gentleness of her face hides a lustful, intemperate disposition. The Law of Moses is very clear on these women."

"The charge is adultery!" said Annas, head of the lower tribunal.

He tapped his fingers and peered down at me. His skin was grayer than his coiled beard; his eyebrows were black and overreaching. He seemed impatient with the proceeding. I sensed no mercy in this man.

"Well, woman," Annas said. "What do you have to say for yourself?"

I stared at the ground.

"Speak, woman. Otherwise, I will have you whipped for impudence to this court."

"Why ask me when you have already determined the verdict?" I felt the anger in my blood. The words had risen to my lips like steam from a boiling kettle.

A murmur of shock passed through the room.

"Who has witnessed my infidelity to my husband that you condemn the child within me?"

Adonijah looked at me squarely. "There is no need to. There is ample evidence from your conduct last night. I am the victim and the primary witness."

I laughed. I could hear it echoing, a bitter laugh so unlike my own. "You read Scripture inside the Temple and indulge your base desires outside of its walls. I am carrying my husband's seed. Why would a woman with child seek relations with a man?" I looked at Annas. "Adonijah of Capernaum, grandson to Jesophat and student to Joshua of Jerusalem, attacked me last night. He led me to a remote place under the pretense of finding Jesus of Nazareth, and my husband. He wanted to obtain from me that for which he would have to pay a prostitute. He wanted to rape me."

Adonijah shook his head. "No! There was a woman drawing water who found us. I would like to call her as witness."

Annas raised an eyebrow, then nodded. "The woman is waiting and willing to testify. Soldiers, you may bring her in."

She entered in a crisp mantle that carried her corpulent girth well. She stood across from me, and her face looked inscrutable.

"Woman," Annas said, "the accused contends that Adonijah, student of the scribe Joshua of Jerusalem, attempted to rape her. Will you testify to that?"

"My lord, I testify to no such thing. I did not witness any coercion."

"Then what did you see?"

"I saw a woman seducing a man."

My eyes widened. A gasp escaped my lips, and it reverberated in the chamber's circular ceiling. I knew that I was doomed.

Annas turned me. "Do you have anything else to say?"

It was futile. I shook my head.

Adonijah smirked. "You see for yourself, revered Elders: her wrath, her viperous lies, and her inversion of

200

truth, the very truth that we hold most dear. Now I ask you to determine the fate of this woman, this Eve incarnate. If guilty, the Law of Moses proclaims death by stoning. Please cast your votes."

Even before the notaries recorded all the votes, I knew the verdict. Unanimous. Guilty. I braced myself for what came afterward. Approaching were the Temple soldiers, military forces at the disposal of the Sanhedrin. I wrung my mantle and clutched at my belly. My child. My poor, luckless child. Then I held out my wrists for the rope that would bind me.

"Wait." Annas paused. "Let us bring her to that Nazarene rabbi. He is in the courtyard of the Temple as we speak. If he does not condemn her, we can arrest him also for violating the Law. That would please the high priest."

I thought I saw Adonijah frown.

———

Jesus was teaching in the Court of Women. A flock had assembled around him, some sixty to seventy followers listening in rapture. I did not see his disciples nearby, even though I hoped to find Simon, who would surely defend me. I saw a child in Jesus's lap, and two other children hugging his calves as they listened, fascinated by his voice. Jesus laughed as the babe in his arms pulled at his beard, the familiar throaty laugh I recalled so often. Peals of laughter burst forth, a tinkling of many bells, as other children joined in the joke. His cheeks crimsoned, and I imagined him as the father of many sons and daughters, running after them in the pasture.

Jesus recognized me. He stood up as the soldiers shoved me before the retreating crowd, creating a rift between my friend and the people. His searching eyes did not leave mine. I saw myself reflected there, a pitiful woman awaiting a death sentence. I shook my head slightly. I was already doomed. I hoped he would be wise in his judgment. I hoped he would save himself against the rage of the Sanhedrin's lower tribunal.

They pushed me until I fell on my knees, and my ankle throbbed as though it was broken. The sand rankled in the wound above my brow. I was becoming death itself; what did a few more scratches and broken bones matter?

Adonijah addressed himself to Jesus. "Teacher, this woman was caught in the very act of committing adultery. Now in the Law, Moses commanded us to stone such women. So what do you say?"

The retinue of Pharisees and elders who accompanied us outside began to pick up rocks. The Temple ground was littered with chunks of limestone and granite, remnants of the last reconstruction of the holy site. Spectators in the crowd muttered "whore," and they too began to arm themselves with stones. I felt the onslaught of saliva; they were spitting on me. A child began to cry.

Jesus bent down and began to write on the ground with his finger. I watched his slender finger brush the earth as tenderly as those he had healed. Enigmatic curves appeared on the surface, words or thoughts or perhaps patterns. I was too far to discern if it was any human language, Greek or Hebrew or even Egyptian, but I didn't care. The gentle consistency of motion entranced me.

"Will you not uphold the Law of Moses?" Adonijah said.

Jesus continued to write on the ground. The air grew still and the people grew silent with expectation. All that was heard was the soft scraping of the carpenter's hand, as if he was measuring the length of a table or the width of the pillar. His concentration felt palpable, as if he traced the fate of humanity onto shallow ground.

"By your silence, do you mean to condone adultery, sir?"

Jesus looked at Adonijah. The scribe's face now appeared to be eclipsed by fear.

"Let the one among you who is without sin be the first to throw a stone at her," Jesus said.

Jesus bent down again and continued to write. He wove his hands through the gravel with an intimacy of a farmer, one who seeded the land and harvested ears of wheat from it. He touched it as if it was a miracle, and I suddenly remembered the living, breathing earth that nourished me, and the bread that satisfied my hunger. Then I remembered that my body was of the earth, it would return to the earth, and there was nothing to fear.

Stone will strike me dead. I looked up, expecting an onslaught. A hush ran through the crowd. Adonijah was white with anger and his hand clutched a large rock, but his fellow scribes restrained him from catapulting his deadly stone at me. Veins bulged from his temples, but the scribes ushered him towards the Court of Gentiles. The mob, armed with shards of limestone and red dolomite, reluctantly lowered their hands. A rumble was heard, the clattering of pellets against hard ground, the clash of stone and earth. Women looked at me grudgingly, stifling accusations and insults they no longer felt justified to hurl. Some spat at me. The crowd began to disband, their thirst for blood dissipated. The Pharisees and priests were storming back into their chambers, rife with frustration. The guards were also marching back into another section of the Temple, their spears glinting. Even the children were gone, carried off by their parents. The dust rose and subsided. There was no one left.

I was alone with Jesus.

He looked at me with that translucent gaze I remembered so well. "Woman, where are they? Has no one condemned you?"

"No one, sir."

"Neither do I condemn you. Go and from now on do not sin anymore."

He understood. His simple words, the kindness of his words seared inside me, culminating in the deepest fiber of my being. He answered the question I did not articulate, and he granted me the forgiveness I had not the courage to ask. I was forgiven. I was released from my bane and my nightmares. I relinquished the dark vestiges of guilt gnawing at my insides. Abba. Bar-Simon. I discharged my hatred for Adonijah. I felt my baby kicking.

I was free. I was still kneeling.

He extended his hand, pulling me to my feet with an assured palm that emanated warmth. For a moment, I sensed a prevailing sentiment of disquiet. It seemed he bore the weight of the entire world on his frail shoulders. His fair countenance betrayed an inner torment; he had aged in recent months, and he no longer seemed young. His eyes, fathomless pools of light, seemed so full that they would spill.

Then I looked into his eyes again. They were the essence of tranquility. I saw an unencumbered love that made me ashamed. I saw myself in his resplendent eyes and I was whole. I was worthy by the sheer fact of being human. He loved me. I had never known such love, perfect and infinite and constant, a love that ached to draw me near.

I followed him.

CHAPTER XIII

Simon had changed in the past six months; there was a wild, barbaric look to his visage. He looked thinner and his face seemed tanner, although his arms and hands were shades more pale. His slate eyes were stony and stern, darkening to an obsidian.

His lips quivered. "You should not have followed me here."

"You should not have abandoned me in Capernaum."

"I had to follow him. I have waited my entire life for this. I feel alive again. Jesus wants to us to be fishers of men, leaders of a New Jerusalem. Founders of a new faith. We will make Israel strong again. We will bring liberation among those under the Roman yoke."

"I came to find you."

"This is revolutionary business, men's work. We are risking our lives here."

"I can help. I am a working pair of hands."

Simon shook his head vigorously. "No. I could never forgive myself if anything happened to you. You belong in the village, where it is safe, where your mother can take care of you, where the Romans cannot attack you in broad daylight. Not on the road with us, not knowing if we will find food or shelter."

His voice became pleading. "There will be dangers. Judas the Galilean was executed. He will not be the last martyr. We are talking about the freedom of Israel. A potential war. Blood and sacrifice. Only men can participate in this fight."

"I have heard Jesus's teachings. I can also contribute to God's kingdom. The poor need to be fed and clothed. I can cook and sew. The sick need to be soothed. I can comfort them. "

I knew I should not cross my husband, even though it had taken great lengths to find him. I spoke involuntarily, as if something within me was bubbling to the surface, another and more obstinate self.

Simon glowered at me. "I tell you, no. Wives must obey their husbands. This is not your calling. This is not your destiny. Jesus has entrusted this mission to us. We are chosen. We are the ones who will die for the cause. You must go."

My husband straightened to his full height.

"I have important work to do."

"What could be more important than your wife and your child?"

"Child?"

His eyes traced my swollen form, the unmistakable bulge of pregnancy. I realized how bloated I must be, my feet blistering from sandals many sizes too small and my tunic stretched out, the threadbare fabric accentuating rather than concealing my condition. His silence was infuriating.

"For the sake of our child, Simon, I came to you. The village wives spun ugly tales with their wagging tongues. There were rumors, and I could not subject our child to their desecrating lies. I want our child to know you." I took a deep breath. I reached forward and closed my hand upon his.

Simon shrank from me and shook off my touch, as if I was a snake. "The New Jerusalem is coming. Have you not heard of the miracles, the wonders, the extraordinary deeds of Jesus? I am his chosen chieftain. We are recruiting new followers. We are changing the world. I do not need distractions now."

"Distractions?" My voice cracked. I strained my ears to ensure I had not misheard. My throat tightened as the blood rushed to my temples. I could feel my face flush. "Is that what we are to you? After you left us in dire straits at Capernaum. All those taxes to pay after the hired fisherman stole your boats and nets. All those malicious whispers, the waiting and watching for me to run away, the madwoman with the bastard child. Then Adonijah and his false testimony. Because of your absence, I was branded an adulteress." I stood there, staring at him. "I have gone through hell to find you."

I did not know how shrill my voice had become. Simon slapped me hard. I was stunned by the gravity of his palm, the stinging of my cheek. I tasted blood where my teeth cut into my mouth. Twice I had been struck by a man.

"You are speaking out of turn, woman!"

My husband glowered at me, his pride a precarious thing he wore on his face, and we were both certain his compatriots had heard us. For once, I did not heed the opinions of others. I blinked back the tears and returned his gaze. His face did not soften. Simon did not speak for a long time.

He stood before me, his hands on his hips. As he shuffled, his dagger and its scabbard became visible. His scabbard sported an unusual design, of coarse white and scarlet yarn wrapped around blue fabric and camel hide. He touched the scabbard before he spoke.

"You will return to Capernaum. You will pack your belongings and leave within a moon of the baby's birth. Your husband commands you."

For an instant, I imagined the arduous journey to the north, the unsympathetic faces of the neighbors in Capernaum. I remembered the sea and my mother and the empty fishing dock. Then I locked eyes with a stranger, a man I did not recognize. He had taken Jesus's invitation as a license of superiority, a unique line of Capernaum men handpicked by the teacher himself. Others were destined to live on the periphery of greatness, glory confined to the rarefied few in the inner circle.

I rubbed my temple, the scratches from Adonijah, and this new injury. My defiant juices were bubbling forth.

I lifted my chin.

"There is a higher command than yours, Simon. Jesus has called me also. I stay as a follower."

———

Despite his imperiousness to me, Simon sought to please Jesus. He was constantly contemplating ways to impress the teacher, having found the intangible to fill the ordinariness of his life. Yet obedience had never been my husband's strong suit. He asked brash questions. He responded impulsively to Jesus without considering his master's meaning. He blundered. In spite of it, he knew this carpenter was the Messiah and did not shy away from proclaiming it to anyone who might listen. His companions revered him for his audacity, and I could see he still yearned for greatness. Here he was called Simon Peter, the formidable rock, and he was no longer a fisherman. Indeed, none of them were.

There were twelve disciples. Many came from Galilee and only the lone revolutionary, Judas Iscariot, called Judea his native land. Sparse in words and volatile in temper, he was the sentinel of the Lord. His face would have been described as noble had the fierce grimace of war not permanently clouded his features. A barbaric look lingered in his eyes, and he carried a sword by his side. Military discipline ran in his blood, and he guarded Jesus zealously. The other disciples lauded him as a patriot, one who pledged total allegiance to Israel's Savior. Simeon the potter—the former Zealot—was particularly reverent toward the Judean warrior.

I embraced the Galileans; these countrymen brought a remembrance of the salty sea air. Andrew had not changed, quiet and compassionate as always. James the colossus had given up philandering with women and sought redemption for his ill treatment of past paramours. John was still the ageless, beautiful boy, but his eyes acquired a humility I had not seen before. Even Levi, renamed as Matthew, left the wealthy life of a publican to chronicle the miracles of Jesus. John often accompanied the former tax collector to receive instruction in letters and language. Thomas the shepherd had also abandoned his flock to follow Jesus, a refuge from his humble trade.

There were others I never met, including the kinsmen of Jesus. Another James, the son of Alphaeus, and Judas Thaddeus were prosperous farmers from Nazareth, each owning nearly ten acres of arable land. Diminutive in stature next to the giant son of Zebedee, Alphaeus's son was known as James the Less. Philip the cobbler and his friend Nathaniel were from Bethsaida, the village of my husband's birth. Nathaniel had left the forge of a blacksmith to follow Jesus, and was praised as a true Israelite, a man without guile.

There were also women. They accompanied Jesus from village to village, providing for his retinue from their own resources. The exquisite Mary Magdalene was a woman of mysterious means. She had become quite famous in Galilee after Jesus expelled seven demons from her body, and it was common knowledge that her fiery heart matched her flame-colored hair. In close company was Joanna, the wife of Herod's steward Chuza. A plump woman with a digestive ailment, she was attended by many servants. Suzanna, the daughter of a renowned silk merchant, gave Jesus thick wool for his mantle, a rare blend of fibers from northern goats beyond Germania.

The company was divided into two quarters: men and women. Jesus, the disciples, and the women stayed in the luxurious dwelling of Chuza, who visited Jerusalem sporadically throughout the year. Joanna offered her home as shelter for the companions and allocated the large inner courtyard to the men, while she retired to the peripheral rooms of the outer courtyard.

Mary Magdalene brought me into the women's quarters, and she nodded at my oversized belly. "You were brave to come such a long way. You must be tired."

I shook my head. Among my brethren in Capernaum, I had become an outcast after Simon's departure. My pregnancy had rendered me a sinner in the eyes of the world. Yet here, even a woman disowned by her father, one who was accused of adultery, was heartily welcomed.

I thought about Mary's story. I wondered if the rumors were true. I marveled at her skin, white as alabaster and so luminous that it appeared she was made of light. Her hair was a remarkable color, for it was not one hue only, but many: dull gold entwined with dark and heavy molasses, lit from beneath with red streaks like sinuous flames. Her slate-gray eyes were disconcerting, and I found myself wondering how many men had lost themselves in their depths.

She smiled at me. "It won't be long now, will it? Perhaps you will be a mother at the next moon." Her voice sounded musical.

I did not know what to say. Then I felt a faint, tickling sensation in my womb.

Mary seemed bewildered.

"The baby is kicking," I whispered.

Her slender hand brushed the surface of my belly, and the child kicked more vigorously. Mary Magdalene laughed with delight, eyelids fluttering, and I saw how very young she was. She was younger than me, and younger than Jesus. She was the indelible flower of youth.

I became even more curious about her past.

———

So I stayed with the women in the house of Chuza. Joanna insisted that I not share my husband's pallet until after the baby was born. "Those menfolk are always poking around, not knowing what is good for the child. They never learn to curb their appetite." Joanna took charge of me and fussed about me like a kinswomen, despite her girth. She chose the ripest pomegranates for me, threatening to boycott the fruit vendors if they gave her anything less than the best. Even the servants were instructed to heap my bowl with the first spoonful of steaming porridge at every meal, to the chagrin of the men.

I followed the women to the Great Temple to hear Jesus teach. The steward's wife could not walk on account of her corpulence; she entrusted the journey to the strength of her litter-bearers. I walked with Mary Magdalene and Suzanna, an unlikely pair: one a flamboyant beauty and the other a spinster considered too homely for marriage. Nonetheless, they walked arm in arm, the merchant's daughter in the middle, Mary Magdalene on the right, and me on the left. Shy in nature, Suzanna spoke little, and it was Mary who chattered away happily. None rejoiced in my upcoming birth more than Mary Magdalene. Surreptitiously rubbing my belly, she believed the soul had already begun to form in the womb, that great seed of intelligence. She believed the words of Jesus would permeate the skin, and that the child would be anointed by the sheer sound of his voice. I listened to the steady beat of my pulsating heart that was beating for two.

We approached the Great Temple and Jesus was already inside, surrounded by eager listeners who prayed for a brush with divinity, a miracle worker, a mystical man, for by now my Lord Jesus had developed a quite a name for himself. We could not get close to him, as the crowds were lawless and each held his vantage point on a first-come, first-serve basis. His voice, potent and prophetic, rose above the din and we listened. I listened to the stories from my Lord. I listened to the richness of his voice. I was learning to listen.

Instead of the usual parables, Jesus grew bold. He taught that God so loved the world that he gave his only Son, so that everyone who believed in him might not perish, but might have eternal life. Those who believed would not be condemned, and those who did not believe were already condemned. He spoke of judgments, of verdicts, and of the light that had already come into the world, but the people preferred darkness to the light, because their works were evil.

He was direct—too direct for the Pharisees and Sadducees and teachers of the Law, who hovered like spies around him. The malignance of their intentions was written in their faces, armed not only with hatred, but with omnipresent Temple guards who were tired of constantly being rallied. I could see their daggers readied at their target, this apparently not being the first time they were called upon for an arrest.

"I am the light of the world. Whoever follows me will not walk in darkness, but will have the light of life," Jesus said.

This proclamation was too much for the Pharisees and the high priests. To insinuate one was the Son of God was heretical. They whispered among themselves hurriedly, conspiring, hoping to find a justification for the arrest they had long been eager to make.

One master of the law, Abithar by name, chose the

troublesome topic of witness to ensnare him. He spoke loudly, so that his voice reverberated throughout the entire treasury of the Great Temple: "You testify on your own behalf, so your testimony cannot be verified."

Jesus gave an enigmatic smile. "Even if I do testify on my own behalf, my testimony can be verified because I know where I came from and where I am going. But you do not know where I come from and where I am going."

Abithar sneered. "How can you be any different from any man here? We all come from woman, and back into the earth we will go. There is still no one to corroborate your claims."

Jesus lifted his hands and examined them. They were working hands, calloused and sunburned, marked by a carpenter's hard labor. Bewildered, Abithar could not help looking at his own hands, the unblemished hands of a priest, shielded from the sun and called upon to write judgments.

"You judge by appearances," Jesus said, "but I do not judge anyone. And even if I should judge, my judgment is valid because I am not alone, but it is I and the Father who sent me. Even in your law, it is written that the testimony of two people can be verified. I testify on my behalf and so does the Father who sent me."

Abithar laughed. "So where is your father?"

"You know neither my Father nor me. If you knew me, you would know my Father also."

Jesus spoke with an assurance so steadfast that the

crowd was visibly moved by him. I watched as Abithar trembled in rage, unable to refute Jesus in this supernatural, circular argument. He gave a signal to the Temple guards, who drew their spears and knives, lunging toward Jesus through the sea of people. They were used to fighting on cue, regardless of the appointed enemy, Roman or Judean or Galilean; the highest virtue of a soldier was, after all, obedience. Their teeth were bared with a predatory instinct. Someone screamed. The crowds scattered like geese before an approaching storm, daggers and metal blades blinking from afar.

Jesus did not flinch and he made no move to avoid the onslaught. He looked at the approaching soldiers with such pity that it spurred them on harder, challenged by a man so oblivious to danger than he made no effort to defend himself. The Temple soldiers laughed at the easy prey, the lamb that would go to slaughter without resistance. The captain thrust his sharpened spear towards the carpenter's neck.

A crackling, the sound of crushing bone, and the captain yelped in pain.

Judas had caught the hand that wielded the spear, his enormous knuckles bulging, and sent the captain backward with such diabolical strength that he tumbled into the guards. Then a quicksilver glint of a dagger and the captain was kneeling, blood trickling from a gash in his leg and seeping into the grainy earth of the Temple.

Judas Iscariot took a step closer to Jesus, his weapon

217

streaked with the ruby red of freshly drawn blood. Behind him stood James the colossus, brandishing a dagger. It became apparent that the loyal followers of Jesus had not scattered; rather they collected behind him like shadows. At the first sign of danger, they made themselves visible, cloaked and bearded, an army hovering over its general. Even my husband bore an ugly, menacing expression that I did not recognize.

Judas raised his dagger again, but Jesus's arm restrained him.

"Spare him. Now is not my time."

Disgusted, Judas glared at the Temple guards, who cowered at his ferocity and glanced questioningly at the captain, awaiting orders. Simeon the potter drew a line with his sword and drove it into the earth, challenging the soldiers to cross the boundary. Indeed, a band of nearly thirty men and women were also beginning to arm themselves with rocks on Jesus's behalf. The pelting was about to begin. The soldiers cocked their heads back and forth like chickens, a dangerous word forming on their lips.

"Riot."

The Judean pointed to the soldiers with his blade. "I have already drawn blood. Don't force me to take lives. Now get out!"

His last utterance rang like a war cry.

———

I had grown ill at the sight of blood, so we hurried away.

When did my husband and the others learn to use a sword? They were civilians: fisherman, farmers, shepherds, and above all, men of peace. They were not soldiers. They had embraced a Messiah who brought love as the universal message of God. What need had they for arms?

"They are trying to kill Jesus," Mary Magdalene told me. "This was not the first time and it will surely not be the last."

I was appalled. Jesus's life was in danger. I felt nauseous, but I bit my lip.

"It is not safe for him to remain in Jerusalem," Mary said. "The animosity of the Pharisees is too great. John, Simon, and Matthew are trying to persuade our Lord to travel back to Galilee, where the influence of the Sanhedrin is waning. There, he would be safe among kinsmen, where bloodlines denote greater loyalty than gold. The Lord would bide his time and gather his followers before returning to Judea. Leaving Jerusalem is a subject of bitter dissension. Not everyone agrees. Judas Iscariot has guaranteed the protection of Jesus with his life, and admonishes any talk of departing. Here, he argues, is where the people need our Lord the most, oppressed under the yoke of the Romans. Here is where Jesus will be the great deliverer like Moses. Jerusalem needs our Lord, because only here can the freedom of the Jews be salvaged." Mary sighed.

A tremor of pain ran through my body.

"Our Lord has not decided," Mary said.

Then she looked at me, her swirling eyes harboring a hint of malachite. I had never noticed it before.

Then I felt familiar vibrations, undulations of the womb. The ground at my feet was wet, a pool of yellow water that I wanted to disappear in. I crouched down to mop Joanna's fine mosaic marbled floor.

"My darling," Mary said. "You are shaking and sweating." She blinked at me and wrapped her fingers over mine. "Oh dear, it must be time. Joanna!"

CHAPTER XIV

All I could smell was the blood. I cried out for my mother. I pushed and pushed, while the old fear reached its insidious hand inside my womb. Joanna crouched in front of me, her steady hands on my shaking knees above the bricks. They said she knew of midwifery, but none suggested she was a midwife herself. Her myriad servants hovered over me, propping silk cushions under my head and pillows under my legs, exchanging anxious glances all the while. Some were changing linens stained a deplorable red. Mary Magdalene held my right arm and brushed my forehead with a damp cloth, cooing soft words of encouragement. Suzanna stood on my left side, feeding me berries and figs, blowing hot whispers onto my face. I tried to blow back, but I choked as the pains came and subsided. Each wave brought intensifying pangs, and the perspiration burned my eyes.

Joanna shook her head. "The baby is stuck."

I head the gasps of horror. It seemed one continuous breath, shuddering from one woman to the next, a travesty none wanted to face. I blinked through the frustration and tears.

Joanna saw me and tried to be brave.

"Darling, I need you to keep pushing."

Mary let out a yelp. "The head…it's stuck!"

Joanna glared at Mary, and the latter was weeping openly, pearly rivulets running down her cheeks. She looked even more breathtakingly beautiful with tears, and the distraction was a welcome one before a lightness entered my head.

"The baby will turn," Joanna reassured me.

Mary was hysterical. "But I can see the toes! All ten perfect toes!" She mourned again and again until Joanna commanded her servants to restrain the whimpering woman, and drag her out of the chamber. Suzanna began praying to Yahweh, her voice melodious and soothing and somber. I fancied a funeral ditty to accompany the passage of a life, hoping it was my own drawing to a close.

So my womb was cursed, trapping the head of my baby. The pain was devastating, and I screamed and wept and pleaded for death. I pushed and pushed until I was nearly faint, the coppery smell of my blood overwhelming my nostrils.

My eyelids grew heavy, and the rich draperies of Joanna's room dissolved. I was too exhausted to struggle with dying, but I thrashed about bargaining with Yahweh for my child. On the periphery, I heard Joanna barking orders to fetch Jesus and the stutter and stammer of protesting servants about propriety and the Law and what it meant to bring a man into an "unclean" birthing chamber. Joanna cursed propriety and cleanliness and asked whether they would rather preserve tradition with blood on their hands from a mother and a child, or break a few measly laws. Urgent footsteps were clambering across the threshold. I heard Joanna calling for a knife.

So this was how my fate would congeal, blood spilling from my womb and burying both of us. I prayed mercy upon the babe whom I would never know. I only hoped that a bargain was made, for Yahweh a covenant once made was eternally binding.

Instead, I heard a familiar voice calling me back. Calling me home.

I opened my eyes.

It was Jesus. He held up a towel and washed my face with rosewater. The scented droplets felt cool and moist on my brow, and the fevered heat of minutes ago seemed to dissipate. Behind him, Joanna knelt, relief written over her face, a knife in her hands. Bereft of speech, I only looked at him and implored. Jesus smiled as he stroked my cheek. Then he placed both hands upon my womb, his touch soft and beckoning.

"The bleeding has stopped. Now you must push."

"But, my Lord," I cried out, "this is unclean."

"Never mind what is clean and unclean. Push."

The pangs came and went, rising in a crescendo of pain, and I pushed and pushed. I longed to expel this boulder, this agony from my body, and I pushed until I thought my eyes would pop from their sockets, my bones would thrust through my skin, and my appendages would dissociate.

A shadow loomed over me, and I saw through my tears that Simon was beside me. He reached for my fingers, but I pulled away as if scalded.

"The baby is coming!" Joanna gushed.

I gave one final push, and like an unfurling, my womb felt empty. An infant's startled screams filled our ears. Mary Magdalene held the glistening, yelping creature, struggling in the abrasive air as Joanna helped me to deliver the afterbirth.

Mary Magdalene fetched clean linens and swaddled our baby within it, cloth the color of salmon against our baby's pinker flesh. She placed the linen bundle into my arms. "Your daughter."

"My daughter," I murmured, dumbfounded, cradling the little one against my breast.

The baby yawned and I saw twin dimples in her cheeks, the rosy pink flesh of a newborn. Her hair looked like whorls of a tended flame…her perfect fingers…her eyelids fluttering in halfhearted sleep … folds of arms and knees. I looked at her long and hard until I memorized every sigh, every feature, her tiny appendages that she did not realize were attached.

She began to cry again, crinkling her face in a propulsion of noise. I was startled by the sound, but Joanna assured me she was only hungry and her tiny lips quickly found her way to my nipple. My breasts were empty, and I now knew the aching every mother felt, the longing for milk that fulfilled the appetite of your babe. I clung to her, even though she snorted in disappointment, as if this was my true purpose for existing, for this child to nestle in my arms. I kissed her head, still wet from the hasty washing, and tufts of hair, fine as feathers. There were no words to describe the way a newborn smelled, fresh and pungent and earthly. Suddenly, I remembered the infant I had lost, Bar-Simon. I wept without knowing whether I rejoiced or mourned.

I heard feet shuffling and looked up to see Simon standing awkwardly beside me, his face a mixture of wonder and perplexity as he gazed down at the tiny creature in my arms. I had never seen such an intense look in his eyes, even when he spoke of Jesus. He reached his arms out for the child, but I pressed her protectively to my chest.

Jesus smiled down at me. I kissed his hands. I would have knelt before him, but the pain pinned me to the bed. No words were adequate, and I struggled to find my voice. Tears of gratitude streamed from my eyes. My body trembled at the remembrance of his touch, a touch that healed, a touch that restored life, a touch that was divine.

"My child, you are healed. The child has passed through the doorway into this life. Be at peace."

Joanna, sensing my confusion, said, "My dear, you were losing too much blood. And the babe's head was stuck in your birth canal until it seemed like both you and the child would burst. I picked up a knife to pry her loose, but I am no surgeon. I began to cut you, to try to widen the path for the baby, but I only made it worse. More blood sputtered from the wound and I feared I would lose you, chastising myself for risking a life when I was a poor midwife and even poorer surgeon. Jesus came at that moment. He touched you, and like an obedient bird, you unfurled, the child spilling into his lap as naturally as to a midwife. He brought you back. Both of you."

Empathy shone in Jesus's eyes, and I wondered if there was anything he did not understand. I opened my mouth, but only stutters came out. A streak of the midafternoon light fell upon his face, and the soft golden brown of his eyes seemed to glow. "Rest," he said simply.

Then he departed. At his cue, Mary Magdalene, Joanna, Suzanna, and all the women left the birthing chamber, and I found myself alone with my husband and daughter.

Simon blinked his wet eyes at me. "May…may I hold her?"

I gazed up at him, trying to remember when I had once loved this man. "I thought she was a distraction to you."

"You…" His brows knitted together. "You said she was *our* daughter."

"Our daughter," I repeated. "Yes, she is yours, but Jesus gave her life. He saved us, while you abandoned us." I turned my head so that I did not have to look upon him.

226

"Do not worry, Simon. I will not be any bother to you. I will stay, but feel no obligation toward me or this child."

His shoulders sagged as if his cloaks suddenly were weighed down by the heaviest of metals. "I did not mean what I said when I commanded you to leave."

"What did you mean?"

His eyes darted from side to side and I could see his anxiety to placate me. "I meant to protect you."

"There is no need anymore." I could feel the fire in my own eyes. "You had forsaken your wife and child when they needed you the most." One arm around my daughter, my other hand reached for the amulet that my husband had offered as a bride price.

"I waited for you for months. Every day that you did not return, I lost hope. I followed you from Galilee to Jerusalem. When you struck me, something in me died. I cannot untie that knot in my heart. I release you from your vows."

I pulled the rose carved in olive wood from my neck. It rested on my open palm, and I gestured toward Simon. He flinched as if he had been assaulted. He backed away from the amulet as if avoiding an evil charm.

"You are free, Simon. Pursue your ambition. Go back to your revolution. Do the work of men to which you are so dedicated."

Simon searched my face for a modicum of sympathy. There was none to be found.

"I will go," he announced finally. "But I will not leave.

You have lost much blood, and you are very weak. I will watch over you tonight."

"There are others who will watch over me," I replied.

For a moment, I thought he might argue, but instead, he turned and shuffled out the door. I did not look at him, although I heard a pause as he stepped over the doorway.

———

I expected a feast on the night of the birth of my daughter, but the ambience was somber and the women refrained from visiting me. I was so tired that only the pain of my baby desperately sucking on my empty breasts kept me from drifting into blissful slumber. After a few hours, my head was spinning and my nipples were sore and chafed. I allowed Mary Magdalene to take the infant from me so that I might steal a few hours of rest.

When I awoke, it was dawn and I was alone on the pallet, but not alone in the chamber. I could see Simon sleeping in the far corner of the room. I watched the uneven rhythm of his breathing. He sat hunched against the basalt wall, his head sagging forward, his hands splayed out on the floor.

The morning glow reflected across his face, mirroring the celestial light ever changing in its moods. It softened Simon's expression; he appeared tired, vulnerable, and capable of remorse. He seemed so old. I could see the fine lines gathering in the corners of his eyes, the strands of gray threading through his dark beard. He was not the optimistic fisherman who took me as a bride so many years ago.

I was no longer that young bride.

I could see my gaunt, bared flesh under the quilts, so different from the lithe figure of my wedding day. I looked down at my hands—no longer soft and smooth, but emaciated and rough. My hair had grown brittle and dry, and perhaps more than my body had been experiencing drought. We had evolved from that beautiful starlit night when Simon had feigned drunkenness to send his guests away and to join his wife. We had been broken by travesty and loss.

Simon stirred on the floor and his eyes fluttered open. Although his face had aged, his unfathomable blue-gray eyes had not. Those eyes were still luminous, full of vigor and excitement and mischief. They were the eyes of a man who wanted to be a hero, a man who rescued me from a miserable fate of loveless marriage. A man who built me an endearing, lopsided bed while he slept on the floor. The eyes of a man who broke convention and endangered his livelihood for love. A man who loved me.

Except he had found something more important than me. Jesus. The promise of a New Jerusalem. Perhaps I was not so different. Perhaps I had found hope in a man who was not my husband. A man who loved without conditions. A man who was the Son of God.

Simon saw that I was awake and struggled to his feet. He held his back protectively as he stumbled toward my bed. His lips uttered my name softly. "You had a restless night. What troubles you?"

I turned my head away from him, not trusting my words.

"Could I get you something to eat?" he asked hopefully. "Some bread?"

"I am not hungry." In truth, I was famished, but I would not allow him the satisfaction of helping me.

"Mary Magdalene will take the baby when you call her," he offered.

I nodded. "Good."

Simon wrung his large hands together. "How long will you punish me this way, woman?"

I summoned my strength to sit up straight on the bed. If I had more strength, I would have left the chamber. "I am not punishing you. I am liberating you," I said quietly. I paused, gazing at my child, remembering the long journey over sand and dust. The anger still rankled in my limbs, like a stubborn ague. "I am relieving you of this burden of a family."

Simon winced at my words. His eyes, those slate gray eyes that were causing a turmoil of emotions within me, watered. "I did not think it would happen again," he said. "I kept away from you because it hurt too much. Even when you followed me here, I did not think that she would survive. Only Jesus dulled the pain. The hope of a new world, a revolution, made me forget."

"That was why you left?"

"Yes." Simon shrank into shadow, shame creeping into his voice. "I couldn't face the pain."

"It was my pain too."

I wanted to relinquish the anger. I inhaled, my chest rising with emotions long suppressed, and a fire ignited within me. I swallowed hard, to temper the words that might burst forth. Simon was not looking at me, but at the baby. He was not ready to conclude his confession.

"It was easier to escape my own failures. I despised myself." Simon hesitated.

"I thought about you often. See," he voice dropped as he gestured to the scabbard of his dagger, camel and indigo cloth, a remnant of my headscarf. It was wrapped with the flaxen yarn that we had spun together so many nights ago. "I carry this with me everyday."

My breasts started to ache, finally filling with the milk that my daughter had been craving the night before. Intuitively, Mary Magdalene knocked on the door to bring me my crowing infant. I placed her on my nipple and felt instant relief as the white liquid poured out of my breast, into her tiny belly. The sound of her suckling soothed me and the anger drained from my body.

Simon approached my bedside and knelt beside me, tousling my hair. He smelled the same as he always did: musky with a hint of salty sea air.

"Almost losing you made me realize how important you are, how important you both are…can we start over?"

I swallowed hard. I hesitated, although I knew he

needed an answer.

Slowly, I shook my head.

"You abandoned me. I do not know if I can forgive that."

Simon looked crestfallen. I bit my lip, repentant for the words that had wounded him. His eyes wandered to the rose carved in olive wood, which lay estranged on the stone floor.

Then I looked down at the infant in my arms. As she suckled, her eyes remained wide open, staring up at me. Deep blue-gray eyes, the color of a tumultuous sea, identical to those of the man standing before me. No matter what he had done or not done, he had given me this miracle. He was her father. We are connected by this tiny life between us.

My daughter's desperate suckles slowed and her lips separated from my nipple as she fell into a peaceful slumber. Simon watched me nuzzle her to my chest, his brow still furrowed. I looked over at him.

"Would you like to hold her?" I asked.

Simon's eyes were incredulous. He was still for a moment, as if he did not know how to react. He breathed deeply. Then he quickly seized his opportunity, fearful there may not be another.

He took the infant from me with trembling hands. He looked at her with such love I had never seen. I realized then that I could never deprive him of this child. Cries erupted from the baby, and his hands lowered toward me helplessly. He coddled her, and slowly she allowed herself to be comforted. She fussed again, her lungs powerful things as she demanded her father to sway her before she would be silenced, as if freed from my womb, she wished to fly.

He gazed on the tawny head and quivering eyelids. He cradled our infant, rocked her from side to side, and the fatigue began to show on his face. Her hand curled around his pinky finger, and then she was slumbering soundly.

"She needs both of us," Simon ventured.

I did not respond. I could not deny this truth, but I had to be authentic to my own heart.

"What shall she be called?" he asked me, never taking his gaze off the sleeping newborn.

I thought for a moment. "As you are Peter, let her be called 'Petra'—the little rock, progeny of our flesh."

Simon looked at me earnestly, and I saw the perspiration glistening on his brow and tear stains along his cheek. I heard the very first words he spoke to our child.

"Petra, my daughter," he whispered, "you are the firstborn of the New Jerusalem."

EPILOGUE

It was for Petra, my sunlit daughter, that festivities followed next, wine and bread and roasting lamb and dates steeped in honey, to celebrate her coming into this world. Strife abounded, passions ran high and the disciples struggled for dominion, for where Jesus would go next. Simon maintained it should be Galilee, where safety was paramount, while Judas Iscariot the warrior insisted on Jerusalem, political hotbed of revolution. I remember the disappointment of Jesus over his disciples, and instead turned to my baby, innocent and unperturbed, to guide his decision. He taught the men to be more like children, and how the nature of newborns was complete surrender. He cradled a child, and called her beloved of God. He proclaimed, "Whoever receives this child in my name receives me, and whoever receives me receives the one who sent me. For one who is the least among all of you is the one who is the greatest." And Jesus decided to retreat to the Sea of Galilee to anoint the babe with the waters of her homeland.

I remember the baptism, a cool splash overwhelming upon infant skin, washing away the inexplicably delicious scent of a newborn. The caravans rumbled on the long journey back to Jerusalem. Somehow, Simon and I began to find each other again. Our story is intermingled with the story of an extraordinary man. In being with him, the ordinary stories of fishermen and wives, tax collectors and disreputable women, warriors and revolutionaries, farmers and blacksmiths were made extraordinary too. I have collected the past like pearls, keeping them safe for you. Be patient, my friend, and I will tell you, when the time comes.

TO BE CONTINUED IN
BOOK II: A FISHER OF WOMEN

ACKNOWLEDGEMENTS

I am indebted to Sara, friend and mentor, who believed in this novel when I faltered, helping me to restructure the plot, refine characters, and understand the world of self-publishing. Many thanks to Kate, who edited multiple drafts and provided insightful suggestions that truly improved the literary quality of this book. I would also like to thank Masahiro Arakawa, who reviewed the text with a scientist's precision and offered perspective into history, context, and general logic. I am also grateful to Paul Nguyen for allowing his exquisite photography to be used in the cover design.

Many thanks to my spiritual teachers and lifelong confidantes, Sister Agnes Bernard Duggan, OP and Dr. Pamela Rauscher, who taught me to listen, pray, and discern.

Thank you to my family and friends, whose love and support, enthusiasm and advice, made it possible to fulfill my dream.

My gratitude to God, for inspiring me with this vision and for the blessing to be an instrument in sharing the message of love.

GLOSSARY OF TERMS

Abba: ancient Hebrew term for father

Amah: ancient Hebrew term for mother

Shomrin: ancient Hebrew term for chaperone

Rapha: ancient Hebrew term for medicine man or woman in ancient Israel

Cubit: measure of height in ancient Israel, approximately 42-48 centimeters or 17-19 inches

Sextarii or sextarius (singular): dry measure of antiquity roughly equivalent to 0.546 liters

Modius: dry measure of antiquity roughly equivant to 9 liters

1 modius = 16 sextarii

Stadia or stadion (singular): measure of distance in ancient Israel, roughly equivalent to 183 meters or 600 feet

Shekel: measure of weight in ancient Israel, also used to express money

1 shekel is equivalent to 11.4 grams or 0.4 ounces of silver

45802015R00135

Made in the USA
San Bernardino, CA
17 February 2017